WITCH

THE CURSED MANUSCRIPTS

IAIN ROB WRIGHT

D1512763

ULCERATED PRESS

Dedicated to the mirror that slashed my palm and forced me to discover the joy of dictation software.

"Childhood is a promise that is never kept."
Ken Hill, Playwright

"By the pricking of my thumbs, something wicked this way comes."
William Shakespeare, Macbeth

"I'm scared to close my eyes, I'm scared to open them! We're going to die out here."
Heather Donahue, The Blair Witch Project (1999), Artisan Entertainment

CHAPTER ONE

THE CRUMPLED Coke can struck the bottom of the aluminium slide and cartwheeled against the playground's metal railing. Ashley had kicked it so many times now that her big toe was numb. If things were any more boring, she might kill herself.

Maybe I'm already dead and this is Hell.

Jude was sitting on the park's yellow-painted bench, flicking a plastic coin into the air and catching it while watching her glumly. His mousy brown hair had grown long over the summer and was hanging in front of his face. "Can you stop doing that?" he asked.

"Stop doing what?"

"Kicking that can around. It's giving me a headache."

Ashley wound up for one last kick and blasted the can across the playground. It struck the overflowing bin next to the gate and bounced through a gap in the railing. It felt like scoring a goal. The afternoon sun bounced off the playground's many shiny metal surfaces and caused her to shield her eyes as she took a seat next to Jude on the bench and looked at him. "What's up with you today?"

"Nuffin'."

Ashley raised an eyebrow. "Liar. You've been having a mardy all day, barely said a word. What's wrong?"

He laced his fingers together on the scuffed knees of his blue jeans and twiddled his thumbs. "I'm just bored. We've been dossing around for five weeks straight, and it's doing my head in. Least when my dad was around, we would go on holiday in the summer, or even just to Alton Towers."

"You miss him? Is that why you're down in the dumps?"

Jude shrugged. "Not really. Been too long now to give much of a shit. I'm bored, that's all, but it makes me wonder what life would've been like if my dad were still around. Never thought I'd say it, but I miss school."

Ashley got off the bench and moved in front of Jude with her hands on her hips. "I'll never be that bored. This year is gunna suck. I've got Mrs Grainger for maths and science. I can't stand that fat bitch."

He chuckled. "Yeah, I used to have chemistry with her. Her breath stinks like shit."

"I can't wait to finish school so we can finally do what we want to do. Two more years and I am out of here. Roll on sixteenth birthday."

Jude spoke in an old person's voice. "And what do you want to be when you're all grown up, young lady?"

She threw out an arm, wiggled it, and let the movement flow through her entire body until it ended in a fancy kick. "I wanna dance, bitch."

Jude nodded in appreciation. "I have to admit it, you're getting really good. Do you dance in front of the mirror in your underwear? You should film it on your phone and send it to *Britain's Got Talent*."

Ashley did a little twirl and flicked another kick that missed Jude's face by only two inches. "I'll take your head off, you cheeky shit." She collapsed back down on the bench. "Anyway, it's you who's gunna go up on *Britain's Got 'No' Talent* with all that magic crap you like. The 'Amazing Jude', that's what they'll call you. You know girls aren't into that shit, right? That plastic coin of yours ain't getting any bitches wet."

Jude shrugged. "Girls ain't into me for a lot of reasons, so magic tricks won't make things any worse."

"God, you're a proper Debbie Downer today, ain't you? If you want to get laid, I'll help you find a lady. There's gotta be a homeless crack addict around here somewhere."

He rolled his eyes. "Whatever. Can we just get out of here, please? My ass is falling asleep."

Ashley nodded. "Yeah, all right. Wanna go to the overpass?"

"Yeah, okay." Jude stood up to join her and the two of them exited the playground through the swinging gate. They took the footpath and headed toward Redsow Woods, the small strip of nature reserve that separated the housing estate from the town's golf course where Ashley's dad used to take her as a child to hit balls. He was always too busy nowadays, but she still remembered how much she used to enjoy swinging a club. It was a good way to work through some anger.

I feel like whacking the shit out of some balls right now.

They kept to the footpath, heading alongside the woods on one side and passing around the playing fields on the other. Eventually, they made it to the overpass, where the footpath spanned a dual carriageway. A tall railing ran along both sides to keep people from throwing themselves off, but there was enough space beneath to dangle their legs over the edge. It was something they came to do sometimes to kill time and watch the world go by. It was one of their places.

Ashley shuffled onto the pavement and slid her legs under the metal barrier. She clutched the bars and pressed her face against the gap, peering at the rushing traffic below. It was a busy road, with cars driving back and forth along it constantly, even at night, even on a quiet Monday afternoon like this one.

Jude scrambled down next to her and threaded his own legs under the barrier. He looked at her and gave a thin-lipped smile.

"Sorry, I'm in a mood today. Just got up on the wrong side. Forgive me?"

"Course, you dickhead. Want to play?"

Jude nodded. "First to ten, yeah?"

"Yep."

The two of them took turns gobbing at the passing cars. If you timed it just right, you could hit the windscreens. There was nothing the drivers could do. They couldn't stop on the carriageway, and even if they could, they would have to climb a steep hill to get up onto the footpath. Ashley and Jude would be long gone by then. Sometimes, the drivers blasted their horns in anger but that only made Ashley and Jude cackle. Getting a driver to beep was worth double points.

Ashley spat a mouthful of phlegm at a passing BMW. "Ooh," she said. "Just missed the bastard."

Jude chuckled, then gobbed a mouthful of spit at a passing motorcyclist. He got the guy right on his bright red helmet.

"Good shot!" Ashley said, whistling. She let a line of saliva elongate and then break, almost hitting a green and white Mini.

"You're useless," said Jude. "I remember when you used to be a challenge. Maybe I need to get a new best friend."

"Good luck. I'm the only person who can stand you. Oh, and your mum thinks you're okay. How is Helen today? Drunk by breakfast?"

Jude rolled his eyes but couldn't keep from smiling. "Shut your face, you nasty cow. She's not that bad, and you know it. Anyway, it's not like she's got any other hobbies."

Ashley pulled at her grubby, shoulder-length brown hair. "Actually, I need to ask her if she can fit me in for a cut. My hair's well minging."

"She's pretty busy at the moment. Everyone's been getting ready for school."

"Good thing I'm best friends with her son then, ain't it?"

"I'll see what I can do."

"Cheers."

They sat for a while, watching the sun descend as the afternoon began its second half. The spitting contest turned out to be no contest at all. Jude got to ten before Ashley even got to five. Three cars had beeped their horns after direct windscreen hits.

Jude cheered up a little, although he started plucking at his rubber bracelet, which was something he always did when he was anxious. "You okay?" she asked, nodding at the yellow band around his wrist. He was halfway through plucking it for a fourth time.

He loosened the bracelet and placed his hands back around the bars. "Just thinking. You know me."

Ashley smiled. She'd been friends with Jude since nursery, where they had bonded over a mutual love of Lego and finger painting. Realising their bond, their mums had started arranging play dates, and they had become inseparable from then on. The problem was that they made no other friends. By the time they had started primary school they had been joined at the hip, and no different when they moved on to secondary. Instead of birthday parties, they went to theme parks together, or pigged out at a Chinese buffet. They spent almost every afternoon after school hanging out at one another's houses. They were like brother and sister, which was strange seeing as Ashley wanted to fuck most lads her age.

"It's getting chilly." Jude rubbed at his shoulders. "Think I might head home and get something to eat."

Ashley nodded. "Yeah, me too."

The two of them pulled their legs back from beneath the barrier and stood up. Evening was still an hour or two away but it was time to call it a day. Five weeks into the six-week summer holidays, the nights were drawing in, which made it more acceptable to go home and chill in front of the TV. At summer's start, after so long at school, it had felt like a crime to go home before ten o'clock.

They were about to get going when Jude groaned.

Ashley turned to him. "What is it?"

Jude turned white as a sheet. He gave a small nod towards the other end of the overpass and Ashley saw what concerned him. She groaned too. "Oh, shit, that's all we need. Come on. Let's get out of here."

The two of them started powerwalking, staring straight ahead and not speaking – trying to hide in plain sight. Lily, Ricky, and the twins were a good thirty metres behind, but it wouldn't take them long to catch up. That would be bad news. Ricky Dalca and Lily Barnes were always bad news.

Ricky and his crew were always dossing around somewhere on the estate but usually near the school or the shopping centre. Ashley and Jude kept closer to home and managed to avoid the local troublemakers most days. Not today, it seemed.

Jude glanced sideways at her, and she could see the anxiety churning inside him. At school, on the few days when Ricky Dalca attended, he always had it in for Jude. Sometimes, Jude faked an upset tummy just so he wouldn't have to go in and face the torture. It pissed Ashley right off.

Right fucking off.

She hated bullies, and Ricky Dalca was the absolute fucking worst. His friends, too.

"Are they following us?" Jude asked, his eyes unblinking.

Ashley dared to peek back, and what she saw made her yelp. Before she had a chance to warn Jude, Ricky rushed forward and shoved him in the back. They hadn't even made it off of the overpass.

We should've run. The bastards were never going to leave us alone. They never do.

Jude staggered and just avoided falling. He spun to face his attacker and summoned a rare display of anger. "What's your goddamn problem, Ricky?"

Ricky was a good-looking lad, which gave Ashley mixed feelings, seeing as she hated his guts about as much as she wanted to snog his face off. Ricky's parents were Romanian, who Ashley's dad said were a bunch of criminals, but he had no accent and didn't look any different to an English lad. He was, however, a criminal. If you needed weed at school, Ricky was the lad to see. If somebody was walking around with a black eye, Ricky Dalca was usually the cause.

Ricky glared at Jude. "*You're* my problem, *Judy*. What 'ave I told you about being outside? I said I'd kick the shit out of you if you left your house, didn't I!"

Jude sighed. He was trembling, but Ashley knew he was doing his best to hide it. "Sorry for needing to get some fresh air. Jesus!"

Ricky stepped up to Jude and glared right in his face. "You don't deserve fresh air, you fucking weirdo. Your mum should make you live in the attic. Fuck, you can't even look at me straight, you freak."

Ricky's friends laughed. The twins hooted in tandem. Lily cackled.

Jude took a step back. "I'm getting laser eye surgery next month, so my lazy eye can finally stop annoying you. Great news, seeing as you bring it up every time we meet. Your concern is heart-warming."

Ashley chuckled internally. If Jude was getting laser eye surgery, he hadn't told her about it.

Ricky scowled and lifted his shaved right eyebrow into a jagged arch. "You fucking cheeking me, mate?"

Jude shook his head and exhaled. "No, Ricky. I just don't know why you have such a problem with me."

Ricky appeared to think for a moment. Then he punched Jude in the stomach and laughed. "Must be yer face," he said.

Ashley stepped in front of Jude to protect him. "Leave him the fuck alone, Ricky. Why you gotta be such a bastard?"

Ricky glared. "Why do you even hang around with this loser? Like, I would never fuck you in a million years, but you can still do better than him."

"You reckon?" Her heart thudded against her ribs. Her fists

clenched in anger. "Because Jude has a massive dick and knows how to use it. In fact, his dick's even bigger than Lily's."

Lily stepped forward. The pale, freckle-covered menace was several inches taller than Ashley, and her wild, frizzy ginger hair cascaded down to her waist like a nest of exotic snakes. She snarled at Ashley. "*You* fucking calling me a man?"

"Think she's calling you a tranny, Lil," said one of the twins, chuckling.

Ashley went to say something, realising she should try and defuse the situation, but before she got the chance, Lily spat right in her face. Ashley reeled backwards, wiping her left eye and cursing in repulsion. "You... you mental bitch."

Jude grabbed her and pulled her back before Lily could do anything else. They tried to walk away, which was probably a smart choice, seeing as they were outnumbered and a mile from home, but Ricky grabbed Jude and shoved him up against the railing. "Where do you think you're going, Judy?"

He hit Jude in the stomach again.

Jude doubled over and gasped. "P-Please, just leave me... leave me alone."

Ricky straightened Jude up against the railing and shoved him back so hard that he struck his skull on the bars. "What if I don't? What if I throw you off this bridge and put an end to your sad little life?"

Ashley wiped the last of the spit off her face and growled in defence of her friend. "I would say the railing is too high. So stop with this bullshit."

Jude was silent. He shuddered and tried to catch his breath.

Lily and the twins cackled. "Fucking do him," said Lily. "I reckon we can get him over the railing."

Ashley saw the pain and fear on Jude's face and could take no more. She threw a punch at Lily but missed, yet it was enough to send the other girl dodging back a step. When Ricky turned to see what was going on, she shoved him hard. He tripped over his own feet and crashed against the railing. The resounding clonk of his head hitting the bars was satisfying, as was his pained tirade of curse words.

Ashley grabbed Jude and pulled him. "Move!"

The two of them took off along the overpass. The others didn't pursue right away, waiting for Ricky to get back on his feet first. It bought Jude and Ashley a few seconds head start.

It had been a while since Ashley had sprinted at full pelt, and it made her realise now how much her breasts had grown. More and more lately, they got in her way, especially when she was dancing.

Street dancers don't have ginormous tits. Why does my body hate me?

Jude was faster than Ashley, probably motivated by the fear of another beating, but he kept looking back and adjusting his pace. Sometimes she wished he would fight back against Ricky – throw a punch – but that just wasn't who he was. Jude wasn't a fighter.

Lily, Ricky, and the twins gave chase, yelling threats. Jude and Ashley had a small lead. The problem was there was nowhere to go. The entire area was closed between Redsow Woods and the playing fields. There were no houses for half a mile.

"They're... gunna catch... us," said Jude, already out of breath. He clutched his ribs where Ricky had punched him. "We have to... lose them somehow."

Ashley looked back at their pursuers. Ricky's face was bright red. He was blowing air out of his cheeks like an angry bull. It wouldn't be a stretch to say that it looked like he wanted to kill them.

Jude searched left and right. He pointed towards the woods on their left. "Let's try to hide in the trees."

"If they catch us in the woods, we're fucked."

Jude didn't give her any choice. His panic caused him to leap into the ditch that ran alongside the path and head for the trees. The woods started with thorny bushes and spindly trees, but things grew thicker after a few metres. Ashley and Jude often trudged through the lighter areas when they were looking for something to do, but she didn't fancy getting cornered inside the woods. At least on the path, a passer-by might intervene on their behalf. Sometimes you could even find the odd community policing officer taking a stroll.

It was a bad idea entering the woods, but Ashley had no choice but to follow her friend.

Jude leapt up the other side of the ditch and dashed between the trees. Ashley hurried in behind him. The two of them dodged through some thick bushes and ducked past the remnants of an old fence.

Ricky leapt into the ditch behind them. "You two are dead," he shouted. "I don't like having to run."

"I'm going to cut your fucking throats," shouted Lily.

Ashley put a hand on Jude's back as they dodged through the bushes. "Keep going!"

Jude dashed to his left. In the direction of the golf course, the woods would gradually thin out, but in the direction they were heading, things grew denser and more overgrown. Countless bushes, branches, and ancient trees intermingled to form a near-constant obstacle course.

"We can't go this way," said Ashley. "We'll break our necks if we keep going."

"What choice do we have? How else will we—" Jude tripped and stumbled forward, landing on his side amongst the thorny weeds. Ashley lifted him to his feet and tried to get him running again, but it was too late.

"Got you!" Ricky moved past them and planted his feet. His gang spread out around them.

Jude and Ashley back-pedalled to where the ground disappeared into a massive drop that the local kids all called Devil's Ditch. Thick bushes covered the ground all around them, but the slope was a steep drop comprising thick mud and hard stone. There was nowhere to go.

Ricky, Lily, and the twins closed in tighter like a pack of hyenas. Ricky glared at Jude, but Lily was grinning. She smirked at Ashley like a hungry serial killer. As much as people around the estate feared Ricky, Lily was the one who truly scared Ashley. The girl's entire family was notorious for being a bunch of thugs – lunatics, really – and Lily's dad was in prison more often than he was out. Both of her older brothers were psychos, and sometimes it seemed like Lily was determined to be even worse. While Ricky still attended school from time to time, Lily had been expelled a long time ago.

Ricky shook his head and chuckled, almost like he was admiring their spirit. "You made me run. I really hate having to run."

Jude put his hands up. "Come on, man. Don't do this."

"Do what? Bury you in these fucking woods? Sorry, mate, but my mind's already made up about that."

Lily stepped up to Ashley, getting right in her face. "And don't think Judy is the only one getting fucked up." She reached into her jacket and pulled out a small length of black plastic. At first, Ashley didn't know what it was, but then Lily pressed a button and a sharp blade flicked out the end. With a malicious grin, she brought the blade up against Ashley's face and pressed the flat side against her cheek. "Maybe I should give you a messed-up eye like your boss-eyed boyfriend here."

"Y-You're not going to use that. Why would you do something so crazy?"

A few steps back, the twins were laughing, but one of them – possibly Danny – said, "Come on, you two. Let's leave these losers to it and go get some beers. We can grab some from our dad's fridge. This shit ain't worth the trouble."

Ricky had moved closer to Jude, but he stepped back now. He looked at the twins. "For real? A'ight, let's bounce and go get drunk. They'll be plenty of time to beat on these losers later."

A wave of relief washed through Ashley's stomach. Perhaps

Ricky and his mates weren't complete psychopaths. They'd had their fun, but enough was enough.

Lily pressed the knife harder against Ashley's cheek. "Nah, I ain't leaving till I see some blood."

Ashley grunted as something bit into her cheek, and she realised Lily had turned the blade and cut her face. She hopped backwards, almost tumbling down the steep slope behind her, and fingered the wound. Her fingers came back bloody. Ashley saw red, literally and metaphorically. "You total fucking maniac. I'm gunna kill you."

Ashley bunched her hands into fists and took a step towards Lily, which she knew was a stupid idea, seeing as Lily still held the knife, but she couldn't stop herself. Rage seized her muscles and mind. She wanted to destroy Lily Barnes. But before Ashley got close enough to engage, Jude tackled her and knocked her backwards.

Then she was tumbling downwards.

CHAPTER TWO

JUDE TASTED EARTH. He spat and wiped at his lips, removing the soil that had wedged between his teeth. The impact when he had hit the bottom of the ditch had rattled his bones.

That hurt about as much as I would have expected.

Less than a knife though.

Shoving Ashley down the slope had been more a reaction than a conscious thought. He'd seen his best friend about to lash out at Lily Barnes, who had been holding a knife, and then, before he even knew what he was doing, he tackled Ashley and knocked her backwards.

I could have broken our necks.

Jude knew he was a coward – and that Ashley didn't understand why he never fought back – but the thought of punching someone made him sick. He couldn't bring himself to raise his fists. At least he had done *something*, though. He had removed Ashley from danger, even if it had required pushing her down a steep slope.

What are friends for?

Jude sat up and looked around. He'd landed on a weed-covered patch of ground, which had softened his fall. Two feet away was a thick, jagged rock that could have caved his skull in.

Shit! Is Ashley okay?

Ashley was lying ten feet away, face down in the mud. She was groaning, which was a relief. Jude realised he was groaning too. His forearms were covered in scratches, and the nerves in his left ankle jolted painfully. He peered back up the slope, estimating that the two of them had tumbled fifteen feet or more. His head was spinning.

He managed to stand. His ribs were still aching from where Ricky had punched him, but the pain was fading.

Ashley stood up too. She patted herself over, clearing away leaves and moss clinging to her clothes. She was clearly pissed off and was just about to say something when Ricky Dalca bellowed from the top of the slope, "You stupid fucking losers! Next time I see you, you're dead."

"I'll cut you properly next time, bitch," Lily shouted.

Jude peered up at his tormentors, wondering whether they would make the perilous journey down after him. When he saw them turn away and leave, he let out a relieved sigh. Lily shouted a few more threats, but her voice faded into the distance.

Jude looked around, seeing nothing but trees, weeds, and mud. It was like they had fallen through time and landed in a prehistoric basin. He wouldn't be surprised if a caveman leapt out at them.

Ashley grabbed him and made him flinch. "You could've killed us, you nutter."

"Lily could've killed you. What were you thinking, trying to fight her? She had a knife."

"She needs to be taught a lesson. She cut my fucking face." Ashley fingered the still bleeding wound on her cheek and grumbled when she saw her own blood. Kicking at the ground, she let out a furious yell. Then she swore repeatedly, using words only beginning with F, S, and C.

Jude put a hand on her arm. "Calm down!"

Ashley whirled on him. "Calm down? Lily's a fucking

maniac. We should call the police. She and Ricky need to be stopped. Those idiot twins as well."

"Don't talk stupid, Ash. Do you remember what happened to Mikey Tanner when he called the police on Ricky last year? Ricky beat his ass so often afterwards that Mikey had to move schools. We don't have it so bad. We just need to avoid them."

"Avoid them? How close to our house do we need to stay just to avoid getting messed with? That crazy bitch cut my face, Jude. I ain't just gunna let that go. Argh!"

Jude took a step forward and examined his friend's face. The cut was long but not deep. "It's not that bad. Just wipe it. It's got dirt in it."

Ashley wiped her face, grunting again when she saw more blood on her hands. After a few moments, the cut stopped bleeding.

"How are your ribs?" she asked.

The mention of his ribs made them ache, but the pain was fleeting. "I'll live."

"Good." She calmed down a little, but when she pulled out her mobile phone, she grew angry all over again. "My fucking screen's cracked. My dad is gunna kill me. Fuck it. Fuck, fuck, fuck it!" She went to toss her phone at the ground but stopped herself, holding on to it and instead kicking the trunk of a nearby tree. Leaves shook loose and rained down around her. There was no controlling her when she was like this.

Jude pulled out his own mobile phone to check it for damage. He didn't have an expensive iPhone like Ashley, so it would be no great tragedy if it broke, but he was still glad to find it intact. He considered calling his mum but didn't see how it could help. Even if he explained where they were, she would never find it. She would probably call the police.

And Ricky would kill us for sure.

Ashley continued to rage, so Jude explored a little. He and Ashley had never entered Devil's Ditch before – everyone said the place was haunted – and if Jude were honest, he'd always been too freaked out to come down here. His mind would run away with him and conjure images of werewolves and monsters dwelling in the ditch.

"Hey, Ashley." He looked at her and frowned. "What's that you've got on you?"

She pulled a face. "Huh?"

He reached out behind her ear to grab something. When he pulled back his hand, Ashley was concerned. "It's okay, I got it."

"Got what?"

He opened his palm to reveal the pretend gold coin. "You're a real treasure, Ashley."

She groaned. "God, is that your latest trick? It would work better if you said you always knew I was made of money."

He tutted. "Damn, you're right. I'm going to use that."

"Just not on me, okay? That trick was lame."

Jude blushed, but before he could get too embarrassed, Ashley pointed back up the slope. "How are we going to get back up there? It's almost vertical."

"I dunno, but we need to wait awhile first. Ricky and Lily could still be up there, hiding. Let's take a walk and see if we can come out somewhere else."

He took a short stroll, glancing back and forth in wonder. While he'd always been too afraid to enter the ditch, now that he was here, the prospect of exploring it excited him.

"Let's head over here," he said, pointing. "I think there's a way through."

Ashley flapped her arms and sighed. While she clearly didn't want to, she followed him, but she complained the whole time. "This sucks. I'm covered in mud. I've got scratches all over my arms. I'm stuck in a ditch. My T-shirt is ruined."

"Just come on, will you? You can take a bath when you get home."

"*If* I ever get home. We're probably going to die out here."

"That's a tad dramatic."

"Maybe."

"Well, even if we do, thanks for telling everyone I had a big dick."

"Don't mention it. I'm sure you do have. Just keep it away from me."

They shared a giggle and then slid through a gap between two thick trees that were wrapped together like embracing lovers. Overhead, the branches were so thick that the sun barely made it to the ground. Devil's Ditch was dark and shadowy, but with Ashley by his side, Jude didn't get too freaked out. Her constant complaining broke the ominous spell and reminded him that life was more boredom than fantasy.

Up ahead, something peeked out of the ivy wrapped around an old oak tree. The object appeared to be metallic, and as Jude got closer, it revealed itself to be an old sign, faded and covered in moss. Only a part of it was visible, and it contained the letters '**RESPAS**'. It only took a moment to work out.

NO TRESPASSING.

"What do you think this place used to be?" Jude asked.

Ashley shrugged. "Nothing. It's a big hole in the ground in the middle of the woods. How could it have ever been anything else?"

"I suppose you're right, but why put a sign out here if there's nothing? Maybe there's a World War Two bunker or an old burial ground like the one they found when they extended the Tesco car park. That would be well cool."

"The sign's probably just to keep idiots like us from breaking their necks down here." She shook her head and pinched the bridge of her nose. "I still can't believe we're down here."

Jude realised she was still seething after her encounter with Lily. If she didn't calm down soon, she'd end up with one of her headaches. Once that happened, she would become unbearable.

"Just chill out, Ash. Everything's fine. We're just having a mooch about, aren't we? Another ten minutes, and we'll try to get out of here. I just don't want another run-in with Ricky."

"I don't know how you can be so calm after he hit you."

"It's not exactly the first time."

"That's my point. When is enough enough?"

Jude sighed. "Just... let it go. It's over now."

But Ashley didn't let it go. In fact, she found a rock, bent to pick it up, and flung it at the sign so hard that she almost went after it. It was an impressive shot, the rock bouncing off the metal sign and ricocheting ten feet into the air. "Now *that* felt better," she said. "Just wish it was Lily's face."

"The warrior princess let loose her sling and struck the evil sorcerer's power stone. The sorcerer's energy ran dry, and with no other option, the wicked monster fled, defeated." He grinned, knowing how much his improvised narratives annoyed her – and yet amused her at the same time. "With her trusted mage by her side, the warrior princess continued on through the enchanted woods, knowing she could not stop until her destiny was fulfilled."

Ashley rolled her eyes and groaned. "Oh please, don't start with your fantasy crap. Not now."

Jude chuckled. One day, he would write an awesome fantasy novel, but for now he was happy just to annoy Ashley, as she always annoyed him with her constant street dance. "The warrior princess thanked her trusted mage for his enduring spirit and unwavering positivity. Without it, she would certainly turn to the dark side."

Ashley grinned, despite her obvious efforts to fight it. "You're such a dork. Perhaps Ricky was right. I can do better." It was only a joke, but it pricked Jude's emotions, and the sudden twinge of upset must have crossed his face because Ashley reached over and gave him a playful shove on the arm. "Hey, I'm just kidding. It's me and you, right? It's always me and you."

"Yeah, I know." He knelt and picked up a withered old branch, whacking it against a tree like a sword and sending vibrations up his wrist. He liked the weight of it but decided not to keep hold of it.

I'm not a ten-year-old anymore.

"Come on, let's see what's over there," said Ashley. She cut left through a gap in the bushes and hopped over a fallen tree trunk. Something scuttled nearby in the undergrowth – a rat or squirrel – and the fact they weren't alone sent shivers along Jude's spine. He followed Ashley, looking around and watching his step, and once again he was in awe of the undiscovered grotto. Based on the overgrown NO TRESPASSING sign, they might have been the first people here in years. The remnants of a barbwire fence snaked through the bushes nearby, but the posts had long ago rotted. Odd bits of concrete lay scattered and pressed into the earth – echoes of the past. It really did make Jude feel like an adventurer on some quest.

"Hey," said Ashley, catching his eye and pointing. "It opens up over here. We might find a way out onto the golf course."

"I think we headed away from the golf course, not towards it. I'm not sure what this place backs up onto."

They pushed their way through a few more bushes, tripping several times on hidden roots and catching their clothes on hidden thorns. Then they made it out into a clearing. What they found was unexpected.

Jude put his hands on his hips and whistled. "Can you believe this? There's something here, after all. How old do you think this place is?"

Ashley moved up alongside him, and they studied the old house together. The building was made of brick, but a third of it had crumbled into dust. Wooden trusses formed its roof, yet only a handful of ancient tiles remained in place. Moss and ivy enveloped the structure, and twisted, intermingling branches made it appear as though the building had grown out of the ground itself.

"It must have been abandoned for decades," said Ashley. "Fifty years, maybe?"

"Try a hundred," said Jude. "I bet this was here before they built the housing estate. It was probably a farm or something."

"It's fucking spooky. I say we get out of here before it gets dark."

Jude moved closer to the farmhouse, stepping through the weeds. "I thought *I* was the cowardly one. You're not gunna wet yourself, are you?"

Ashley rolled her eyes and shook her head. "Dick."

The old farmhouse intrigued Jude. Again he thought of how the two of them might be the first people to set foot here in years. It excited him. None of the local kids knew about this place, so in a way, it belonged to him and Ashley. It could be their secret getaway.

He automatically took another step forward, as though he were being pulled by some invisible chain. It was only when his foot came down on something soft and yielding that he stopped. "Oh, are you kidding me? Gross!"

"What is it? Badger shit?"

Jude started wiping his trainer on the weeds, knocking loose a layer of moss and revealing dark brown mud beneath. Lying in the undergrowth was what looked like a dead squirrel. Its midsection was split open and worms thrashed in its guts. The blood had dried, but tiny silver bones were visible. A faint, unpleasant odour drifted from the corpse, enough to turn Jude's stomach. "It's a dead squirrel, I think."

Ashley wrinkled her nose. "That's comforting. Maybe we should say a few words out of respect. Hey, now that I think of it, if I die before you, I don't want music at my funeral, okay? I want a beatboxer." She put a fist against her mouth and started putting out a beat. It was one of her many talents, and every few seconds, she stopped to spit a few lyrics. "Lily Barnes has got an STD. She'll suck your dad's dick and do it for free. Ricky Dalca is a Romanian bitch, too scared to follow if you run into a ditch."

Jude chuckled. "If you get famous, promise me you'll release that track."

Ashley pop-and-locked, her body writhing as if it had no bones. Although it sometimes grew annoying, Jude had to marvel at his friend's dancing skills. He found it difficult just to touch his toes.

Ashley stopped dancing and grinned at him. "After the diss track I'd lay down on Lily Barnes, she would never show her face again. That shithole family of hers will disown her."

Jude stepped over the dead squirrel and approached the farmhouse. He still couldn't take his eyes off the old building. It was large, and it beggared belief that such a place could go abandoned and unnoticed for so long. Especially when there were families nearby living in tiny houses and dinky flats. Jude couldn't imagine living in a place like this, with so much space.

"I want to go inside," he said.

Ashley shook her head and took several steps back. "No way. You go in there and the roof'll come down on your head."

"There isn't a roof. And I don't think the building is suddenly going to fall down after so many years. Come on, who knows what we might find. There might be antiques."

"Antiques? Are you serious? The place doesn't even have four walls. It's empty. Abandoned. Dangerous."

Jude walked towards the farmhouse. "The mage feared no danger, for his faith in the almighty gods would keep him safe."

"The mage has lost the plot."

He ignored Ashley's protests and carried on, knowing she would eventually follow him. They always backed each other up, and it had got them this far in life, so why change a winning formula? One down, two down, they always said. When trouble found them, they faced it together and shared the consequences.

The unpleasant odour Jude had detected around the dead squirrel was worse as he approached the farmhouse. It was a sickly odour, like opening a fridge to week-old chicken. It wasn't unbearable, but it filled Jude with a mild sense of dread about what he might find inside. More dead squirrels? It was enough to make him turn back.

"Wait up," said Ashley, and she hurried up behind him just as he approached a gap in the wall where a front door might once have been. "Can we get out of here after this?" she begged him. "This place gives me the creeps. And it stinks."

"Yeah, okay. Ricky and Lily should have gone by now. We'll have to climb our way back up the slope somehow, but at least they didn't follow us."

Ashley huffed. "Bunch of pussies, the lot of them."

"Yeah."

Jude headed up a couple of old brick steps that were still in place. The mortar had cracked, and they formed an uneven V shape rather than a flat surface. All the same, they took his weight as he stepped on them and entered the doorway.

Inside the farmhouse, it was even darker than out in the ditch. The roof trusses cast a grid-shaped shadow over the stony floor, and in several places, the ancient tiles had cracked. Weeds and vines grew through the gaps.

Ashley stepped in behind Jude and grunted. "See? There's nothing here."

Jude was disappointed. His overactive imagination had promised forgotten treasures – old trinkets and history made manifest – but all he found was a crumbling brick room with a broken stone floor. The only thing of note was an old brick fireplace with a length of old timber running across its top. At some point, it might have been a living room. Now it was empty.

Jude continued forward.

"What are you doing?" asked Ashley. "This place isn't safe. We should just leave it be. God, how can you stand the smell?"

"Just let me check one more room, okay? There's a door here." And there was. The wooden door was hanging from the opposite wall at an odd angle, still attached to a pair of ancient hinges. Most of the frame had rotted, but there was a room beyond. Jude couldn't help but walk towards it. Ashley continued complaining, but, as always, she went with him.

Jude put a hand against the edge of the door and felt it move. When he pulled on it, it was stiff, wedged against the stone floor. The understairs cupboard in his house was the same way, so he knew what to do. He placed a hand against the top edge of the door and pushed, tightening up the hinges. Then, when he pulled again, the door moved easier. It dragged across the stone floor and made an unpleasant sound.

Jude hurried into the next room, hoping to find something more interesting than in the last. Like the room preceding it, it was made from brick and tile. It was empty except for one thing.

Jesus Christ.

CHAPTER THREE

Ashley bumped into Jude and made him yelp, but his sudden shock was almost entirely from the sight of the woman kneeling on the floor in front of him. It was so utterly unexpected that his breath caught in his throat and he failed to speak.

Ashley, being made of tougher stuff, was less silent. "What the fuck? What the actual fuck!"

A woman was imprisoned in the centre of the room, chains attached to her hands and ankles. Apart from a thick gold locket hanging around her neck, she was completely naked. Jude immediately hated himself for examining her unwashed body, but he couldn't help it. She was beautiful beneath all the grime, with long blonde hair and bright blue eyes. Jude had the sense of her being wounded, but he couldn't work out where.

Strange markings covered the room. Symbols on the walls and floors.

"We have to help her," said Ashley, her words clipped and breathless. "We have to help her."

Jude reached out a hand to the woman. Whoever she was, she was clearly in a bad way. But as soon as he did, she shrieked at him like a wild animal. She thrashed at her chains and tried to bite him. Her eyes bulged.

What the hell?

Ashley and Jude stumbled back through the doorway, crying out in terror.

CHAPTER FOUR

"Jesus fucking Christ!" Ashley put her hand on Jude's arm and yanked him back into the previous room. All the while, the naked woman screamed. Jude was screaming too, totally freaking out. If she didn't calm him down, he'd go into a complete panic. The problem was, she was fucking freaked out too. In fact, she had to cover her ears to block out the woman's wild screaming before it sent her mad.

Jude stopped screaming long enough to form a few words. "This is fucked up. This... This is fucked up."

Ashley knew she would have to take charge, so she grabbed Jude by both arms and shook him. "Listen to me! We can deal with this, okay? Let's just..." She shook her head. "Shit! I don't even know what this is. You're right; it's fucked up."

Jude turned and looked back into the other room. "She won't stop screaming, Ash. What the hell is wrong with her?"

"What the hell do you think is wrong with her? Some sicko had stripped her naked and chained her up in the woods. She's probably been, I don't know, abused and that. I need you to calm down and think this through with me. Don't freak out on me, Jude, please."

Jude gave her a skittish nod. His breathing was shallow and

rapid, but he attempted to get a hold of himself. After a few seconds, he nodded at her again. "I-I'm okay. We need to help her. Hold on..." He pulled out his phone and dialled. Then he pressed his lips together and moaned.

"What is it?"

"I don't have any reception. I can't make a call."

Ashley tried not to panic. "Okay... that makes sense. We'll have to carry her out of here and call for help as soon as we can get a signal."

Jude nodded, white as a sheet.

Ashley stepped back into the other room. The woman glared at her, still screaming. She thrashed against her chains, more like a wild animal than a human being.

Has someone kept her here so long her mind has gone? Is it too late to even help her?

Ashley put her hands up and spoke softly, then realised there was no way she would be heard over the screaming. She had to raise her voice, which made it hard to sound soothing. "We're not going to hurt you. It's okay. You're safe."

Jude stepped into the room behind her, echoing similar assurances. "We're going to get you out of here. My name's Jude. This is my friend, Ashley."

The woman finally stopped screaming. Ashley felt the pressure leave the inside of her skull and sighed with relief. The piercing shrieks had actually been causing her pain. Now that she was quiet, the woman stared at them. Her bulging eyes were bright blue, but bloodshot. Beneath the caked dirt and sweat-streaked grime, she was beautiful. Ashley would happily trade her own rapidly growing breasts for the woman's supple, modestly formed ones. There was barely an ounce of fat on the woman.

When did she last eat?

Why the hell is she here? Who did this to her?

There was a rancid stench in the room, and she wondered if the woman had been going to the toilet, but when she looked around, she saw nothing gross. No shit on the floor or buckets full of piss. In fact, the only thing on the floor was some strange dark brown markings. The largest was a thick triangle in the centre of the room. The woman knelt in its centre. Several smaller shapes covered the surrounding floor, as well as the walls, but they made no sense to Ashley – just random lines and squiggles. Nothing obvious revealed the cause of the smell other than the woman herself, but Jude clearly noticed it too because he held the crook of his arm over his nose and his eyes were watering.

Ashley dared take another step. The woman flinched like a cornered animal. She had stopped thrashing at her chains, and they now lay slack against the stone floor. Ashley looked for a keyhole but couldn't find one. Then, suddenly horrified, she realised the chains were attached directly to the woman's flesh. Her hands had been mutilated, the chains running straight through her palms. Likewise, a second chain pierced the backs of her ankles in a continuous loop kept in place by a steel bracket on the stone floor. Ashley put a hand to her mouth as her stomach did a nauseous backflip. "This is bad," she mumbled.

Jude followed her line of sight, and she gave him a moment to figure it out for himself. He, too, covered his mouth in revulsion.

The woman looked down at her ruined hands, then back up at Ashley. She seemed to stop noticing Jude altogether, and although she didn't speak, Ashley saw pleading in her bloodshot blue eyes. The woman had clearly been through hell. Ashley had no doubt about the cause.

A man. Only a man would do this.

Ashley knew the world was more dangerous than her parents and teachers let on. Television alone was enough to show that certain men were predators; sick-minded monsters who viewed women as playthings. She realised now that they were standing in the lair of one of those very men.

What if the sicko comes back and finds us?

This is bad. Very bad.

"We have to get out of here," she said.

Jude looked at her. "What?"

Ashley shook her head, knowing that she was being anything but courageous. She was, however, being rational. "We need to go get help. There's no way we can free her. We're not capable of dealing with this. What if the person responsible comes back?"

Slowly, Jude's eyes widened as he obviously realised what she was saying. They were in terrible danger, and they were only a pair of kids. Let the police handle things.

"You're right," said Jude, although he seemed sickened by what they were deciding. He turned to the chained woman and took a step towards her. "Listen," he said softly, crouching down in front of her. "We're going to get help. We'll be back, okay? I promise you, everything will be fine."

Ashley suddenly felt like an animal in a trap. She wanted to run – her heart was begging her to – but she couldn't go without Jude. "Come on! We need to go. Right now."

"One second." Jude reached out a hand to the woman. "We'll be right back, okay? Just try to—"

The woman sprang forward, lengthening her chains until they stopped her at the edge of the painted triangle. She snapped her teeth at Jude, trying to bite his face. Jude screamed in fright, recoiled, and lost his balance. His arms went out behind him and he crashed against the wall. A piercing cry escaped his lips.

Ashley rushed to gather her friend to his feet and pulled Jude away from the thrashing woman. He groaned and held his hand against his chest as she pulled him back into the other room.

Ashley's heart was beating a mile a minute.

The woman started screaming again.

Jude had clearly injured his hand, so Ashley grabbed his wrist and forced him to show her. His palm was bleeding from a nasty gash that ran from the edge of his wrist towards his thumb. Ashley winced as she noticed something sticking out of the wound, and before Jude noticed, she pulled it free. It appeared to be a small piece of plastic, but she couldn't see a way that there could be any plastic inside a derelict old farmhouse.

Is it a shard of bone?

Jude gasped. "It hurts."

Ashley threw the piece of bone to the ground before he saw it and tried to set his mind at ease. "It's nothing, just a cut. You must've landed on something sharp."

"I want to go."

"Me too. Let's get out of here. Whatever's happened to that woman, she needs more help than we can give. We have to call the police."

Jude put his wounded hand by his side and shuddered. He looked like he might throw up. "So... So we're going to leave her here for now? Alone?"

"What else can we do? Sooner we leave, sooner she gets rescued. Come on!"

The two of them fled the farmhouse.

It was strange, but the clearing around the farmhouse seemed different. The trees and bushes felt closer. There was less moss and undergrowth on the ground; and a lot more mud.

Ashley panicked when she failed to spot a way out, but got a hold of herself once she located the gap in the bushes where they'd entered. She pointed it out and Jude nodded. They wasted no time hurrying away from the farmhouse.

The woman's screams escaped the open roof behind them.

In the short time they'd been inside the abandoned building, it had grown darker. While it was not yet night, dusk had arrived and things had grown colourless. The green leaves were dark. Tree trunks appeared grey.

Ashley's mind was spinning. She was in a horror movie, running through the woods after making a grim discovery. Once again, she feared whatever sicko could chain a woman up and leave her.

Jude stopped at the gap in the bushes and pulled aside the

branches. She'd never seen him so pale, but he was keeping his shit together. It must have taken great effort because panic was one of his default modes. A few years ago, Jude had been trapped in a lift with Ashley and had gone to pieces. By the time someone had got the lift working again, forty minutes later, he had been sobbing in her arms. It was embarrassing, but that was Jude. Her best friend was 'sensitive'.

The two of them fled the clearing and headed back towards Devil's Ditch. She still didn't know how they were going to climb back up the steep slope, but for now she was glad to be running. She exerted herself so much that she barely noticed the pain of the brambles, thorns, and branches whipping at her. Her only focus was on pumping her arms and legs. Jude was one step behind her, mumbling under his breath as he ran. It sounded like he was trying to comfort himself. Maybe he was doing his adventurer thing.

The warrior princess and her trusted mage escaped the sorcerer's pit, leaving behind a tortured slave.

Nope, it doesn't make anything less scary.

That poor woman.

Who is she?

They made it out of a swath of thick bushes and reached the bottom of the slope. Seeing it again now sunk Ashley into an even deeper pit of despair. It looked twice as high as before and even steeper. How on earth had they avoided breaking an arm falling down it?

"How do we get out of this ditch?" she asked. "It's too high."

Jude skidded to a halt, kicking up a patch of moss. He scanned the ground. "There has to be a way. Let me think. Let me think. Just let me—"

He was panicking.

"I'm here with you, Jude. You're okay. We just need to get up this slope."

Jude almost stared right through her, but he found his focus and nodded, letting her know he was calm. He searched the immediate area, grabbing sticks and tossing them aside, picking up stones and examining them. Ashley didn't see how any of it was helpful, but there was no point denying that Jude was smarter than her. If there was a solution, he was most likely to find it. So she waited.

After a few minutes, Jude made an excited sound. He grabbed a thick branch buried in a bush and pulled it free. It had fallen from a nearby tree. He hunted a moment more and found a second thick branch of a similar length. He handed it to Ashley.

She shrugged. "What do I do with this?"

"Let me show you." He took his branch over to the bottom of the slope and held it in both hands. Then, as if he were catching trout in a river, he speared the branch into the mud. The ground was firm, but the branch was sharp enough to plant itself. Jude used it to steady himself and clambered up the steep incline. Once he was in line with the branch, he dug in the toes of his trainers and yanked it free. He repeated the process two more times, planting the branch higher and higher. He looked back at Ashley and grinned. "It's easy."

Witnessing the effectiveness of Jude's method, Ashley hurried forward and planted her branch into the slope. Jude was already ten feet up. She didn't intend to get left behind, so she moved as fast as she could. While it hadn't rained in a few days, the mud was wet in places where the thick tree canopy had obviously blocked the sun from making it onto the slope. Once she realised that, she made rapid progress.

Kiss my arse, Devil's Ditch.

She looked up and realised Jude was about to reach the top of the slope. Happy to know that at least one of them was safe, she held onto her branch and took a breather. She waited until Jude made it up onto the flat ground above and then gave a muted cheer.

Then he disappeared from sight.

Ashley waited.

Then she worried.

"Jude? Jude, what are you doing up there?"

For a moment, she feared he'd run off without her, which would have been unlike him. *One down, two down*; they always had each other's back. To prove her point, Jude reappeared, peering down at her and waving. "I was just checking for Ricky and Lily. I was worried they might still be up here. There's no sign of them, though."

"Good, because I'm in no mood for their shit."

Jude clapped his hands together, then wagged a finger in a beckoning gesture. Ashley suddenly realised she was hanging from a branch ten feet in the air, so she got moving again. She planted the branch in some wet mud a little higher up and clambered upwards. Twice more, and she was at the top of the slope.

God, I can't wait to get out of this ditch.

Jude stretched out an arm. "Grab my hand. I'll pull you up."

Ashley nodded. She held onto the branch with her right hand, reached out with her left.

Crack!

The branch snapped in the middle, and suddenly she was standing on the steep incline with no support. Gravity seized her, begging her to fall backwards. She yelled out, knowing that whatever happened next was going to hurt. Her eyes met Jude's. His mouth was as wide open as hers.

Their hands met.

Jude grabbed her, barely in time to stop her falling. He yanked her up over the crest and onto the flat ground. Ashley collapsed onto her knees, panting, while he patted her back. "I got you," he said. "You're fine."

"That would have sucked so bad." She looked up to thank him but noticed his hand was bloody. There was blood all over her wrist, too, but it wasn't hers. "Shit! Jude, your hand! You used it to grab me."

Jude examined his bleeding palm. "Huh... It was instinct. It doesn't hurt that bad anymore. Come on, let's go."

Ashley got to her feet and the two of them took off. They headed through more snarled undergrowth and nigh impenetrable bushes, but at least this time they knew the way ahead was going to get easier. Soon enough, they reached the lighter part of the woods.

They decelerated and walked for a couple more minutes, catching their breath and avoiding the pratfalls that running entailed. It felt good to be back in the world they knew, not far from the footpath. Ten minutes and they would be home. Then they could call the police and let somebody else deal with this – a grown-up. For the first time in a long time, Ashley was glad to be a kid.

She put a hand on Jude's back and sighed. "This is so messed up." She laughed at the absurdity of it. The ordeal had only happened fifteen minutes ago, but it already felt like a dream. No way could there be a forgotten old farmhouse that nobody knew about. No way could there be a naked woman chained to the floor.

No way.

Chains right through her goddamn hands and ankles.

For fuck's sake. Did that actually just happen?

Jude chuckled, too, although it was high-pitched with anxiety. "This is going to blow up," he said. "As soon as the police find that woman, things will explode."

Ashley hadn't thought about it, but she realised he was right. There would be a massive investigation, as well as a manhunt for the sicko responsible. Ashley and Jude would probably end up in the papers, or even on TV. Maybe they would get called heroes, but Ashley could already imagine the crap she would get at school for this. Everyone would want to know all about the naked lady in the woods. The thought of so much attention threatened to bring on a headache.

The footpath appeared through the trees, a light grey shape against the darker hues of the wood. They sighed in unison, then walked in silence for another minute until they broke free of the trees. They stepped down into the shallow ditch that now seemed little more than a divot and then onto the pavement. The feel of concrete beneath Ashley's muddy trainers was reassuring. She enjoyed the sound of her footsteps on solid ground.

The playground was a short walk ahead. They were almost home, and despite still being freaked out and moderately terrified, Ashley felt her body loosening up. Her heart no longer hammered against her chest.

She turned to Jude. "You okay?"

He nodded. "I am now. Just glad we got out of those woods. It's getting dark."

"Yeah, we only just made it. What time is it?"

Jude pulled out his mobile phone and looked at it. "Eight fifteen. Should I call my mum?"

Ashley shook her head. "I don't think we can do this over the phone. Let's get home first. We'll go to yours. My dad will only freak out. Let me enjoy a few more hours of him not knowing about this bullshit."

Jude nodded and put his phone away. They carried on until they reached the playground, then both of them froze.

Ashley looked at Jude and mouthed a single word, "Shit!"

Ricky, Lily, and the twins were all sitting in a line on the playground's painted metal bench. Their backs were turned from the footpath. From the way Ricky was hunched over, Ashley assumed he was rolling a joint. The smart thing would be to run the other way, but then how would they get home? They could make a call to get her dad to collect them, but she really didn't want to deal with him yet. Also, Ricky might spot them and give chase anyway. Then they would end up even further from home.

Deciding she wanted Ricky and his gang behind her rather than between her and Jude's house, Ashley put a finger to her lips. Jude nodded to show he understood, and the two of them crept forward. While Ricky and his crew focused on what they were doing, they might not turn around. If they did, however,

Ashley wanted the chase to be in the direction of home, not *away* from it. She just needed to get on the other side of the playground before they were spotted.

Ashley could hear Jude's hurried breathing and wondered how loud her own breaths were. Was she breathing loudly enough that Ricky would hear them? She didn't think so, and slowly, she started to believe they might manage to creep past.

Then: "Hey!"

Ashley and Jude froze. Ricky got to his feet and turned to face the footpath. He had a smirk on his face, knowing he'd caught them.

"How was Devil's Ditch?" he asked. "Did you suck each other off down there? You should have fucking stayed."

Lily stood up too. Her eyes narrowed when she saw them standing there on the path. "Wanna see my knife again?"

Ashley shoved Jude in the back. "Run!"

They legged it. Ashley's body was already aching, sick to death of climbing, running, and fleeing, and her breasts, as usual, caused a hindrance, but she made it past the playground. She dared to look back and was relieved to see Ricky sitting back down. He was laughing, and he obviously couldn't be bothered to give chase. He and his mates probably didn't want to abandon their weed. Even so, Ashley and Jude didn't stop running for a hundred metres. By then, they were both out of breath.

Ashley had a stitch. She clutched her ribs and doubled over. "This has been like the worst day ever," she said.

Jude helped her to stand straight and held onto her as they resumed walking at a steadier pace. "Tell me about it."

Five minutes later, they made it to Jude's house. His place was smaller than hers, a narrow slice of windows crammed between two other homes. It had no downstairs toilet and only two bedrooms, but he lived alone with his mum, so it didn't really matter. His garden, however, was much larger than hers, so they hung out at his more than they did hers. Also, his mum, Helen, was really laid back.

They opened the front door and rushed into the hallway. Jude's mum was standing in the kitchen, watching the small LCD hanging on the wall and pouring herself a glass of wine. She placed the glass on the counter when she saw them hurrying inside. With the raising of an eyebrow, she gave them a crooked smile. "What's got into you two?"

The words came out all at once, Ashley and Jude both speaking at the same time. Jude showed his mum his cut palm, which sent her immediately into a panic. It was almost like she hadn't heard them about the naked woman chained up in the woods, but once she realised Jude's hand wouldn't fall off, she calmed down and listened. Two minutes later, she was on the phone with the police.

CHAPTER FIVE

"It won't be long now," said the tall Asian man who had introduced himself as PC Riaz. The police officer was sitting in Jude's kitchen, sipping from a coffee mug with a picture of 'Del Boy' Derek Trotter on the side. He'd arrived fifteen minutes ago and had immediately made a call for his colleagues to search the woods. While the officer's willingness to believe their story should have filled Ashley with confidence, it only caused her anxiety. Several police officers were frantically rushing about now because of her, and it felt like trouble. She eyed the back door that led to the garden and thought about running. A stupid idea.

Jude was bent over the kitchen sink while his mum cleaned his wounded palm, which upon closer inspection was quite nasty. The gash was short but deep. Now that things were calmer, Jude was fussing about the pain. "It hurts, Mum."

"I know, honey, just let me get it clean." She wiped sweat from her forehead with the back of her arm and blew a strand of straight blonde hair out of her face. Her roots were showing, which was unusual. She also seemed tired, and Ashley wondered if she was a little bit drunk.

"Mum! Ouch!"

"I'm almost finished. Just— Oh, honey, your bracelet's gone. I don't remember the last time I saw you without it."

Jude glanced at his naked wrist. "It must have come off when I fell." He tutted. "Damn it."

"It's only a cheap rubber bracelet, sweetheart. Never mind."

Ashley saw the sorrow on her friend's face. It hadn't just been a bracelet. It had been one of his many crutches. Even now, she could recognise his urge to pluck at the tight yellow band.

"So," said PC Riaz, looking at Ashley, "tell me again what you two were doing in the woods?"

With Jude and his mum busy, Ashley was the only one who could answer the officer's questions, so he focused on her. She cleared her throat and shifted in her chair. "We were bored. Sometimes we like to go exploring."

The officer raised an eyebrow. "Exploring?"

"Yeah. There ain't much else to do, is there? Anyway, we didn't realise we'd gone as far as we did. We just kind of ended up there. Are we in trouble?"

Helen peered back from the sink. "Of course you're not, love. You two are heroes. That woman owes her life to you."

PC Riaz nodded. "It's private property and you shouldn't have been there, but I think we can excuse that. This woman is going to have a lot to thank you for. Can you tell me anything about her? I know you've tried already, but while we wait to hear from my colleagues, it might help if we keep talking."

Ashley tapped her fingers against the table and avoided making eye contact. The memory of the woman in the farmhouse made her shudder. She'd been in such a terrible state, yet there had also been something oddly terrifying about her. She'd been wild and aggressive. Dangerous. "I think she was pretty," said Ashley. "Blonde hair. Blue eyes. Like, *really* blue. She was, you know, naked – but she still had this locket around her neck, which was kind of weird. Oh, and there was blood, I think, but

I'm not sure from where. It could have been her hands. The chains went right through them."

"Oh my," said Helen.

PC Riaz frowned. "The chains pierced her hands?"

Ashley nodded. "And her ankles. It was horrible."

"I can imagine. You've certainly been through a lot today. What about the room the woman was in? Anything you can remember about it?"

"It was empty. The only thing I saw were these strange markings all over the floor."

"Markings?" PC Riaz leant forward, placing his elbows on the table.

Ashley and Jude hadn't yet mentioned the strange markings on the floor and walls of the farmhouse. Truthfully, it just hadn't come up. When they'd first spoken with the officer, only the bigger picture had seemed to matter. Now the smaller things felt important. "There were these weird symbols on the floor," she said. "The woman was sitting inside this big triangle. It was weird. Also, when Jude cut his hand, there was, like, a chunk of bone or something stuck in his palm. I pulled it out."

Jude groaned and turned away from the sink. "Ash, you never told me that! There was a chunk of bone in my hand? Gross."

PC Riaz looked at Jude. "Perhaps you should visit the hospital, young man. Don't want to get tetanus."

Helen grabbed him and gave him a squeeze. "He'll be fine, officer. He has his old mum to look after him. I cleaned the wound. Just need to get a bandage on it." With that, she started rooting around in the kitchen cupboards. She was acting frantic, moving quickly and clumsily.

PC Riaz returned his gaze to Ashley. "These symbols? Do you know what they were? Were there any words?"

Ashley shook her head. "No. Just lines and circles, stuff like that."

"They were like magic symbols," said Jude. "The type of thing you see in witchcraft."

PC Riaz didn't appear to find it absurd. He didn't laugh and remained deadly serious. "And what do you know about witchcraft, son?"

"Nothing. Only from, you know, films and that. The symbols looked like hexes or spells. Arcane sort of stuff."

Helen grabbed a bandage from a tin, and with a bemused *tut,* she grabbed Jude's arm and pulled him over to her. "That's enough of that, you. Sorry, officer, he has an overactive imagination. He wants to be a famous magician one day, don't you, sweetheart? You should see all the tricks he has in his room, ha!"

Jude blushed.

"He's really good," said Ashley, seeing how embarrassed he was. He never did magic tricks for anybody except her. "And he's right. It could have been occult symbols we saw. They were weird, whatever they were."

PC Riaz took a sip of coffee and placed the mug down on a chipped wooden coaster. His radio was on the table and he stared at it for several moments. Ashley looked at it, too, wondering what would eventually come from the other end. Would the officers find the woman alive? Or would she be dead? She and Jude had left her alone out there, chained up in the woods. They had run away and left her. The sicko could have returned and murdered her, knowing the police were on their way.

One of us should have stayed.

I was too afraid. I was too afraid to stay.

I'm a coward.

"I'm sure we'll hear something any minute now," said PC Riaz, possibly sensing her unease. "Oh, I haven't asked you, how did you get that cut on your face? Did you fall inside the farmhouse?"

Ashley froze, knowing the truth would do her no good.

Involving Lily Barnes wouldn't help the situation. "I, um, caught it on a branch while we were running away. I didn't even notice, so can't say exactly when."

PC Riaz nodded.

"I'll get a plaster for you, sweetheart," said Helen. "Just as soon as I'm done with Jude."

Ashley waved a hand. "Don't worry about it, Helen. It's fi—"

The radio on the table squawked. Everybody flinched. PC Riaz snatched it up and thumbed a button on the side. "Okay, go."

"We found the farmhouse," said a voice on the other end, "but there's nothing here. Nothing at all."

PC Riaz frowned. His eyes fell upon Ashley as he replied into the radio. "Did you check every room?"

"Affirmative. The whole place is a ruin. There's nothing here. Only thing we found were a few footsteps in the dust and a bracelet.

"A bracelet?"

"Yeah. A yellow rubber thing. It was lying right in the middle of the floor."

"Any symbols on the floor?"

"Symbols? No, not that I've seen. The place is derelict. There's nothing here."

"Copy that. Spend ten more minutes on site, then return to base. I'll catch up with you at the station, Steve."

Ashley was already talking, fumbling for words, but not knowing what on earth to say. She had gone through several outcomes in her head, but none had ended this way. "Th-The sicko must have come back! He must have moved—"

PC Riaz put up a hand to silence her. "I don't know what you two are playing at, but I had you pegged as good kids. Whether you got some kind of scare, or your imaginations got the better of you, this is unacceptable. I could arrest you right now for wasting police time."

Jude moved away from his mum, an unsecured bandage flapping from his hand. "The woman was there! We're not lying. I swear. Mum, I swear."

Helen rubbed at his back and nodded. "I believe you, sweetheart." She looked at PC Riaz. "Your men must have the wrong place. My son wouldn't make this up."

PC Riaz shook his head and sighed. He seemed as much confused as he did angry. "Unless there's another abandoned farmhouse where your son lost his bracelet, I think we found the right place." He looked between Ashley and Jude, scrutinising them. "Honestly, I don't know what to make of this. I want to give you kids the benefit of the doubt because I can't see why you would make up a story like this, but this doesn't add up. Look, I'll file your statements tonight and do some research about missing women matching your description, but I think the two of you need to have a good long talk and decide how you want to proceed. We found your bracelet, Jude, so there's no doubt my colleagues found the right place. This doesn't look good, does it?"

Jude averted his eyes and muttered, "No."

"So where is this woman you've told me about? Where's the blood? Or all of these occult symbols you both mentioned?" Ashley went to speak, but PC Riaz cut her off again with his palm. "Sleep on it tonight, okay? Perhaps we can have a different conversation tomorrow. I need the night to decide what to do about this."

"Surely they're not in any trouble?" said Helen.

"I can't promise that, ma'am."

"She was there!" said Jude, teary-eyed.

PC Riaz's placid expression broke, and he put on a scowl. "Don't dig yourself in any deeper, son. Get some dinner and go to bed. We'll revisit things in the morning."

Ashley grunted, and under her breath, she said, "This is bullshit."

Helen shushed her. "Ashley."

PC Riaz tilted his head as if he hadn't heard. "I'm sorry, young lady?"

"I said, this is fucking bullshit. There was a woman chained up in that farmhouse. Jude and I aren't lying. She was there. She was fucking there. Instead of doing something about it, you're talking to us like a pair of naughty little kids."

"I suggest you calm down, right now."

Ashley jumped up from her chair and slapped the table. "She was fucking there, so why can't you find her?"

Jude was shaking his head and staring into space. "We left her. We never should've left her."

PC Riaz looked between them. Once again, he appeared as confused as he did angry.

"You need to find her," Ashley yelled. "You need to tell your stupid mates to search that house properly and do their fucking jobs."

PC Riaz downed the last of his coffee and slammed the 'Del Boy' mug on the coaster. He stood up from his chair and clicked his fingers at Ashley. "Okay, young lady. I was willing to put this down to some kind of mischief gone wrong, but my good faith has dried up. I'm taking you home to your parents. They should be made aware of your behaviour tonight."

Helen moved towards the table. "Come on now, Officer, there's no need for that. I'll see that Ashley gets home safely."

PC Riaz looked past her and focused on Ashley. "You can either go in handcuffs or by choice, but do not test my patience. I've none left. You've had half the station running around for you tonight, young lady, so either you calm down and come with me, or I'll be calling your parents to come and collect you from the police station."

Jude groaned. "Just go with him, Ashley. Just... go."

Ashley was furious. It took everything she had to keep it all inside and not make things worse. She had known this would end with her somehow being in trouble. She had just known it.

"Fine," she said, shaking her head. "Take me home. With any luck, I'll only get grounded for a year."

Worse luck, and my dad will chain me up like that woman in the farmhouse.

She was there.

She was real.

We saw her.

CHAPTER SIX

Ashley's dad was furious, which was nothing new. He kept snatching at his jet-black hair and yanking it so that it tufted out at the sides and made him look insane. He paced back and forth in the kitchen. Now and then he would pick something up, like the coffeepot or a ladle, and stare at it as he spoke. It was as if he couldn't bear looking at Ashley.

Ashley was leaning against the kitchen counter, staring at her bare feet and twinkling her toes. "I've told you," she muttered. "It's the truth. There was a woman in the woods."

Ashley's mum put a hand over her face and groaned. "Ash, you need to stop this. You're going to end up in so much trouble. I know the summer's been boring, but this isn't right. You can't tell lies like this."

Her dad put the ladle down and finally looked at Ashley. "I'm so disappointed in you, Ashley. I didn't raise a liar. This isn't why I work so hard."

Ashley's hands clenched into fists. She kept focusing on her toes, trying to stay calm. It was difficult. "Why don't you believe me?"

Her mum spluttered. "The police said there was nothing out there. How *can* we believe you?"

"How about because I'm your fucking daughter."

Her dad pointed right in her face, his heavy gold bracelet catching the kitchen's spotlights. "Don't you dare use that kind of language under my roof. In fact, get to your room. I can't even deal with you right now."

Ashley sneered. "Fine!" She stomped towards the kitchen door. "Thanks for nothing."

"I'll bring you something to eat," her mum called after her.

Ashley stomped into the hallway and started upstairs, making sure her feet pounded every step. Her heart was thudding against her chest again, and as much as she wanted to punch the walls, she also felt a flood of tears coming. She didn't understand what the hell was going on. How could such a mundane, boring day end up this way?

She went into her bedroom and pulled out her phone. The screen was cracked, but she could still see most of the display. She pulled up her short list of contacts and called Jude. He answered after only two rings.

"Ash?"

"Yeah. You okay, Jude?"

"Not really. This doesn't make any sense."

Ashley chuckled without humour. "Tell me about it. That woman was there, wasn't she? She was real."

There was a slight pause before Jude answered. "There's not a doubt in my mind, Ash. That woman was chained up."

"So where the hell did she go?"

"She must have... that... somewhere."

Ashley pressed the phone against her ear. "What did you say? I didn't catch that."

"I said... that... must have... where."

"Dammit. The signal is bad. Can you hear me? Jude, are you still there?"

There was a beeping sound, and when Ashley looked at her phone, the call had ended. She thought about calling him back but decided against it. She just wanted to lie back on her bed and stare at the ceiling. Her mind had been running a thousand miles a minute for the last few hours and she was exhausted. No more thinking or talking or moving.

She threw her phone on the bed and perched on the end. Her sheets had been changed, and she could smell the scented dryer sheets her mum used. The duvet cover was pink with little rainbows on it, one she'd had for years. It suddenly seemed childish. Likewise, her purple-painted walls annoyed her, and she wished they were just plain white. The things in her room that had once given her comfort now only made her sad. The stuffed unicorn on her windowsill that her dad had won from a grabber machine on a day trip to the seaside now only reminded her of how old she had got, and how she could never go back to those carefree times of being a child.

My dad doesn't look at me the way he used to. I'm not his little girl anymore.

She listened to her parents arguing downstairs and tried to make out the words. As usual, it was her dad's voice which was loudest. He was ranting and raving about everything and nothing.

What else is new?

She didn't know if he had always been this angry, or if it was just lately, but she hated being around him. He was constantly grumpy. Perhaps it was his job – he never stopped going on about how much he hated it – but she wasn't even sure what he did, other than it was at a factory. He often came home covered in oil and would spend a full hour in the bath with a glass of wine. Often, he would say that it wasn't who he was supposed to be, like he was being forced to work against his will. If he hated his job so much, he should just quit. Maybe then he would cheer up and be her old dad again.

I miss him.

When Ashley had been a little girl, her dad had always told her he would one day open an Italian restaurant and let her work in it with him. Her grandfather had owned a restaurant in Italy before she'd been born, and it was her dad's dream to do the same in the UK. The older she had got, however, the less her dad talked about the restaurant and the more she realised dreams didn't come true. Now, even if he did open a restaurant, the last thing she would do was work there.

For a while, she sat on the end of the bed in total silence, staring at herself in the mirror attached to her rickety old wardrobe. The scratch on her face had scabbed over, and her hair still had bits of twigs and leaves in it. She looked like a lunatic.

Maybe I'm crazy.

Maybe I imagined the whole thing about the woman in the farmhouse.

But Jude saw it too.

Lost in thought, she flinched when her bedroom door opened. It was her mum, holding a tray with a plate of sandwiches and a packet of crisps. "Your dad was going to make spaghetti," she said, "but he's too stressed now. If you get hungry later on, there are Pot Noodles in the cupboard."

Ashley thanked her mum and took the plate of sandwiches. "Has he calmed down yet?"

"Don't be unfair, Ash. He has a right to be angry. We're both really disappointed in you."

"But *you* didn't lose your shit, did you, Mum? Why is he like this? He never used to be."

Her mum tutted. She picked up Ashley's phone from the bed, turned around, and sat beside her. "People have different ways of dealing with things, honey. Your dad has reached an age where he's *analysing* things a little too much. He wanted better for us than this – he has a lot of dreams – but the world is tough and it's hard sometimes. Give your dad a break, okay? Things will go back to normal soon. Anyway, I'm surprised you're judging him so much, seeing as you two are so alike. You have a temper as well, Ashley."

Ashley nodded. She was aware of her own temper and wished it wasn't there, but it was just part of who she was. She took things personally, and it was obvious why. Like her mum had said, Ashley and her dad were the same. Italian temper: that's what he always called it.

When Ashley didn't reply, her mum patted her on the leg. "We'll sort all of this out. I'm not sure what happened today, exactly, but I know you're not a liar, Ash."

"Really? You believe me?"

Her mum nodded. "Yeah, I suppose I do. We'll sort it all out tomorrow, okay? Once your dad has calmed down, we can deal with things properly."

There was a banging downstairs, followed by the sound of Ashley's dad stomping around in the kitchen and shouting.

Ashley's mum sighed and stood up from the bed. "He must've dropped a wine glass. I'd better go help him. Here's your pho—" She had been about to hand Ashley back her phone when she noticed the cracked screen. "Oh, Ashley, you've only just got this. Your dad's going to have a fit."

Ashley reached a hand out, begging for the phone. "Don't tell him then. It's fine. It still works. I'll just have to live with it."

Her mum put the broken phone in her jeans pocket. "I'll take it to the market tomorrow and see if the phone man can fix it. Perhaps your dad doesn't have to find out. Now, eat your sandwiches."

Ashley smiled. "Thanks, Mum."

Her mum left her room and closed the door. Ashley remained on her bed and ate the sandwiches – turkey and mayo, her favourite. The fact that her mum believed her caused her temper to finally take a breather, and things felt a little easier knowing that not everyone was out to get her, although she was still utterly confused and pretty freaked out. There were still tears gathering behind her eyes but, as she concentrated on eating, they slowly went away.

Then she stopped eating.

She froze with a mouthful of turkey sandwich because it

didn't taste like turkey. In fact, it didn't even feel like turkey. Something was off.

Wrong.

Her teeth had bitten into something hard and fibrous.

Grimacing, Ashley leant over her plate and spat out the sandwich. For a moment, she didn't know what she was looking at, but then something in the half-chewed mush wriggled – half a worm. There was blood mixed with the white bread.

"Jesus Christ!" Ashley leapt up from her bed and threw the plate on the floor where it broke in two. She started spitting and wiping at her mouth. "What the fuck? What the actual fuck?"

Heavy footsteps sounded on the stairs. Ashley clenched her fists and waited for her dad's arrival. He burst into her bedroom, already angry. "What the hell is all the racket and shouting?" He noticed the broken plate on the floor.

Before he got a chance to yell again, Ashley cut him off. "There's a fucking worm in my sandwich. What the hell, Dad?"

It took him off guard, and some of the anger slipped from his face. He looked down at the sandwich, frowned, and prodded it with his foot. "What are you talking about?"

"A worm. Look! It's right..." Ashley stared at the sandwich but couldn't locate the half-eaten worm. She dropped onto her knees and pulled the bread apart.

No worm.

"I... I..."

Her dad huffed. "Do we need to get you a doctor, Ashley? Seriously, what the hell is wrong with you?"

Ashley shook her head in disbelief and didn't know what to say. She felt like she was dreaming.

More like a nightmare.

Equally as perplexed, her dad shook his head and let out a sigh. "Just... clean this up. I don't want to hear from you for the rest of the night."

"Fine."

She waited for him to leave, then cleaned up the sandwich. Still no sign of any worm.

I'm losing my mind.

There was no worm.

Maybe there was no woman.

I can't think about this anymore. I'm going to have a nervous breakdown.

If I haven't already.

She reached down and pulled her laptop from beneath her bed, wanting to occupy herself. Netflix, YouTube, whatever; she just needed something to quieten the whispers in her head. She hopped onto her bed and lay back against the pillows with the laptop across her thighs. Opening the screen, she started browsing for something to watch. Eventually, she decided on a comedy. Right now, she needed to laugh.

She pressed play on some random romantic comedy that came up in her recommendations and settled down to watch it. After a few moments of watching a black screen, she tapped at the spacebar. With the way her night had gone so far, her laptop breaking would be the cherry on the cake. Fortunately, the film started playing a moment later, although it wasn't what she expected.

Rather than some peppy music over a top-down view of some city, or a melodramatic coffee shop break-up, the film opened with two children playing chase in a field. They were wearing old-fashioned clothes. One of them, a boy, even wore a flat cap. The girl wore a frilly cream-coloured dress. The two children were running around, chasing one another outside a lovely old house. In fact...

What the hell?

...it was a farmhouse not unlike the one Ashley had visited today. It was enough of a coincidence that she reached for the escape key, but before she could close the window, the two children turned to the camera and let out an ear-piercing scream. The camera zoomed in on their faces, and all Ashley could see was their pained expressions. It was a shock, and she barely kept from tossing her laptop away and wailing in fright.

Instead, she fell into complete silence.

Her mouth fell open in horror as the children's faces began to wither and rot before her eyes. Their skin burst open. Their cheeks melted away. Worms wriggled from their noses and mouths. Their eyeballs shrivelled away inside empty sockets.

I'm going to throw up.

Ashley slammed her laptop closed and tossed it onto the end of her bed. She wanted to scream out for her parents, but she knew they wouldn't believe her. They would only lecture her for watching inappropriate films, and she didn't want to hear any more of her dad's ranting tonight.

She was alone with her terror.

I'm alone.

She slid beneath her bed sheets and wrapped herself up tightly. She stared up at the ceiling, too spooked to look anywhere else.

I'm going insane. I'm going insane. I'm going insane.

CHAPTER SEVEN

Jude's tummy rumbled. Checking his watch, he saw it was nearly nine o'clock. With the drama of the evening, his mum had forgotten to cook. It wasn't the first time, but at least this time she had a valid excuse.

He had been surfing the web on his laptop, considering whether or not to masturbate, but he decided he wanted food more. He slid his laptop under his bed and went downstairs. The lights were all off except for the lamps in the living room, and when he peeked in, he saw his mum spread out on the couch. A bottle of wine sat, empty, on the coffee table in front of her, and she was watching *Judge Judy*, murmuring to herself and chuckling. Commentating on television programmes was a habit of hers after a few glasses. Last month, they had sat and watched *Wreck-It Ralph*; he'd barely heard a word.

Not even sure who the villain was.

Jude continued into the kitchen and switched on the light, then went straight to the fridge. He rooted around, but there wasn't much in. He scrounged a yoghurt and a lump of cheddar, which he cut into thin slices and put in a sandwich. Luckily, he wasn't a big eater. He'd make up for it in the morning with a big bowl of cereal. He sat at the kitchen table and ate.

What a freaky day.

I hope Ashley's okay. Her dad probably went schizo when she got home with a police escort.

Jude liked Ashley's parents, but her dad could be a little scary when he was in a bad mood. He shouted a lot and stomped around the house. Ashley's mum was always nice, though. She had used to be good friends with his own mum, but they had fallen out about something three or four years ago. Neither would say what about.

The cheese in his sandwich was hard, which he hated – the taste too strong – but he kept eating because he didn't want to go to bed with an empty stomach. Most nights, he watched TV or played a video game until around midnight, but right now he could barely keep his eyes open. He didn't think he'd make it past ten. Of course, there was a good chance he would lie awake all night, worrying about the trouble he was in. PC Riaz had said he intended to speak with him and Ashley again tomorrow.

He said we were wasting police time.

But we weren't lying. The woman was real. She needed help.

She needed our help, and we left her.

Jude finished two-thirds of his sandwich and paused. He leant over the table and spat out the contents of his mouth. Grimacing, he decided the cheese was too hard and tangy for him to bear, so he opened the bin and slid the remains off his plate. Then he grabbed a spoon from the cutlery drawer, gobbled the yoghurt, and poured himself a small glass of water. Finished, he headed back out into the hallway, where he heard his mum speaking a little louder than before. He looked in again and saw her on the phone. She was likely talking to one of her girlfriends, of which she had many. Unlike Jude, his mum was a social butterfly.

"He's going to be the death of me, that boy," she said. "I don't know what's wrong with his head. Naked women chained up in the woods? I mean, can you imagine how embarrassing it was, standing there in front of a police officer while my son goes on about witchcraft and naked ladies? You're right, Val, absolutely. Maybe I do need to take him to see a doctor."

Jude's tummy sloshed with an emotion he couldn't quite name. It was wrong to eavesdrop, and truthfully he didn't want to hear any more, so he hurried back upstairs. Ashley would have kicked off if she'd caught her parents talking about her like that, but once again he was inadequate in his response. Instead of getting angry, all he felt was loneliness. His own mother thought he was nuts. Either that or a liar. He didn't know which was worse. Lying wasn't something he did, yet, somehow, everybody was doubting him. It wasn't fair.

He felt himself getting anxious and didn't want to go to bed all het up, so he decided to run himself a hot bath. It was something he often did to calm down. Hot water never failed to soothe him.

The drab grey bathroom sorely needed a refit and had for a while. The bath panel was missing, exposing the pipework beneath, and the lino was ripped in several places. His mum had neither the money nor skill to sort the room out, but even in such a bad state, it was still Jude's favourite space in the house. At least the taps worked, and the scalding water filled the bath without complaint.

Stripping naked, Jude rubbed his shoulders against the chill. Eager to get warm, he perched on the side of the bath and placed his feet in the water. It made him shudder. Streaks of dirt lined his ankles and the points of his elbows, put there by his gambol down Devil's Ditch. His body ached, his shins covered in bruises.

Once the bath was half-full, Jude slid off the edge and slipped beneath the water. Another shudder escaped him and he lay back to relax. He tried to shut his mind off and think of nothing, focusing on the water's calming caress. Suddenly, things didn't seem so overwhelming. There might be trouble ahead, but at least he knew in his own mind that he had done nothing wrong – plus whatever happened probably wouldn't be as bad as he feared. It rarely was. PC Riaz seemed like an all right guy. Surely he wouldn't take things further than they needed to go.

And there's no reason to worry about Mum. She'll wake up tomorrow with a hangover and barely remember any of it.

Once again, Jude fretted about Ashley. She hadn't seemed herself lately. She was... angry. More so than normal. It upset him, seeing her get so mad at the drop of a hat, and truth be told, she scared him sometimes. His best friend had always had a temper, but not as bad as lately. The worst part was he didn't know how to help her. He didn't even know what her problem was. They had used to share everything, but recently it felt as though Ashley was keeping things from him, almost like she didn't trust him anymore. No, that wasn't right; it was more like she didn't think he would understand. Maybe he wouldn't.

Jude shivered with the cold and then frowned because he was submerged in hot water. It took a moment to register, but he realised the water had gone cold. In fact, it seemed to be getting colder by the second.

What the...?

Jude leapt out of the bath, shivering and grabbing at himself. He took a towel from the radiator and wrapped it around himself. Then he stood there, confused. The water had been hot when he'd sat with his feet in it. It had been warm when he'd slid into the bath. No way could it have turned so cold so quickly. It was impossible.

Impossible.

Maybe mum didn't pay the gas bill?

Jude padded back over to the bath and dipped his fingers into the water. It was so chilly that it made the bones in his hand ache.

Lovely and warm one minute, icy cold the next.

He yanked back his hand and shook it, then considered racing downstairs to tell his mum. But what could he possibly say?

She'll end up booking that doctor's appointment for sure.

So he got himself dry and hurried across the landing with the towel wrapped around his waist. There were no answers to the questions plaguing his mind, so he slid beneath the bed covers and grabbed the TV remote, intending to distract himself. Switching on his old 32-inch that he had got for his ninth birthday, he lay back against his pillows and tried to relax. Perhaps now might be a good time to finish *The Hobbit* films. It would either take his mind off things or send him straight to sleep. Either was fine.

The opening credits of the second movie began to play. The instrumental music was calming and Jude zoned out as the camera focused in on a lush green meadow. Two children played in the tall grass. Their mother stood nearby, watching them. They all wore old-fashioned clothes. It had been a few days since Jude had watched the first movie, but this didn't seem like the sequel at all. His confusion grew when the scene continued without context. The mother marched over to the children and pulled something from underneath her skirts. The object flashed in the sunlight but moved too swiftly for Jude to identify.

Is that...?

Is that a knife?

Jude recoiled in horror as the mother started stabbing her children. The scene was more realistic than any he'd ever seen. Blood spurted into the tall grass. The children's old-fashioned clothes darkened with leaking fluids. The mother's face was expressionless as she stabbed them again and again and again, a hundred times each. By the time she finished, their bloodless bodies had melted into the earth.

Jude grabbed the remote and switched off the television. He wanted to scream. He wanted his mum. But he realised he was alone. He tried to call Ashley, but there was no answer.

I'm alone.

And I'm going insane.

CHAPTER EIGHT

Jude didn't know how long he'd been asleep, but the fact he was struggling to open his eyes suggested it hadn't been long enough. He had spent most of last night staring at a fixed spot on the ceiling and trying not to freak out. The image of the slain children was pasted to the back of his eyeballs and he couldn't shake it. He could smell their blood. But in the early hours of the night, his body must have overridden his mind and sent him to sleep. He was grateful for that.

Now it was a new day, and the night's terror ebbed away. With the gift that only sleep provides, Jude was now partially detached from the previous day's events.

The fires of yesterday are ashes today.

Destiny dies and renews every second.

Jude reached into the drawer of his bedside table and pulled out a pad and paper. He jotted down his thoughts, wanting to capture them for the fantasy book he was one day going to write. The pen he used resembled a magic wand, a gift from Ashley. She had found it for him during a holiday in Wales.

He pulled on jeans and a T-shirt, then went downstairs. It was half-past ten, later than he usually woke up, but his mum hadn't shouted up to him or tried to stir him – it was the summer holidays, after all. He found her in the kitchen, emptying the bin. Glass bottles clinked inside the black bag, and Jude wondered how much she'd drunk last night. Her bleary eyes and frizzy hair suggested too much.

Why does she do it to herself?

Jude and Ashley shared the odd bottle of cider now and then whenever they could convince an adult to get it for them, but truthfully he didn't much enjoy the sensation of being drunk. In fact, the smell of cider alone was enough to make him queasy. The last time they drank cider, Ashley had ended the evening puking in the middle of a field. She'd been so miserable that she'd begged him to kill her. It was overly dramatic, but that was Ashley. Life was never boring with her as a best friend.

"Hey, sweetheart. How's your hand?"

Jude had forgotten about his palm, which was good in that it hadn't caused him enough pain to notice. Now that he looked at it – and flexed it – it ached, but not too badly. He wondered what it looked like beneath the bandage. "It's okay. Can I have some cereal?"

"Of course. You know where it is."

Jude rolled his eyes and went over to the cupboard. "Yep, I know where it is."

His mum took the black bag out to the bin cupboard while Jude made himself a bowl of cereal and sat at the table. As his mind woke up, he pictured the two dead children. He was certain it hadn't been *The Hobbit* playing.

So what the hell happened? What the hell did I watch?

And then there's the bath water. How did it turn so cold?

Jude's mum came back into the kitchen and poured herself a coffee. Jude hated the stuff and only drank tea. She never offered to make him one, so he got up and made one for himself. Then he resumed eating.

His mum sat, sipping at her coffee. "You look tired," she said. "Didn't sleep well?"

Jude dropped his spoon in the bowl and shrugged. "Not really. I was a bit freaked out after everything that happened."

"I can imagine. Have you thought any more about what happened? Perhaps it would be better to have a different story ready when the police come back."

The recollection of hearing his mother talking about him on the phone last night came back and hurt him all over again. She didn't believe him, and even thought he needed professional help.

"Like what, Mum? What should I tell him? That I'm crazy?"

She leant in her chair and frowned at him. "Of course not! But maybe you should say you didn't actually see the woman. That it was Ashley who did, and that she just convinced you."

Jude examined his mum's face, trying to work out if she was kidding. She'd known Ashley for ten years. "Are you for real? I would never stab Ashley in the back. She's my best friend. Jesus, Mum."

She put her hands up as if she meant no offence. "Okay, okay! Look, I understand she's your friend, but she's also a very troubled young girl. Hardly surprising with that dad of hers."

"What does that mean? What's wrong with her dad?"

"Nothing. Forget I said anything. All I'm saying, sweetheart, is that you have a brain in your head – you can make something of your life – so don't let anybody else drag you down by involving you in their problems."

Jude let his head hang and went back to eating his cereal. After what he'd heard his mum say about him last night, he was in no mood to listen to her advice. Ashley was his best friend and had always been on his side – one down, two down. What they saw yesterday had been real. His mum might be right about telling another story to the police, but it was something he needed to talk to Ashley about first. If they changed their statements, they needed to change them together.

Jude stood up. "I'm going out. I'll be back later."

His mum nodded. She never objected to him going out, and

she never told him when to be back. He appreciated it most times, but this morning he wondered if she even cared.

"Uh, one moment, you," she said. "Clean your bowl first."

"Oh, yeah." Jude snatched his bowl and took it over to the sink. Whenever he was over at Ashley's, her mum waited on her hand and foot, but he was lucky if he ever got a hot meal. Sometimes, he wanted to yell at his mum to do better. But he never did.

Jude cleaned up his cereal bowl and headed out into the bright sun of a cloudless morning. After a stuffy and sleepless night, it was nice to be outside, breathing fresh air. The sound of birds, and distant cars on the carriageway, made his problems seem smaller. The old man who lived across the road was cleaning his old blue Rover. He waved when he saw Jude. Jude waved back.

Focus on the little things. Focus on the moment.

He went to pluck at his bracelet.

Damn. I dropped it at the farmhouse. The police have it. Wonder if they'll give it back to me.

Jude left his close and headed where he always did – to Ashley's house. She lived on a nicer road than him. Her house had a garage and driveway, which was useful because both of her parents actually drove. His mum had never even taken lessons.

Dad drove, though.

The memories of his father had faded, the pages of a book left in the sun, but he remembered a small red car. He remembered days at the zoo and supermarket trips. Then... the memories just stopped involving his dad. There was a line in his brain – before and after.

He picked up the pace, eager to meet up with Ashley. He wanted to tell her about the strange events of the prior evening. She needed to hear about the icy bathwater and the strange, horrific scenes that had played on his television. She was the only person in the world who would believe him.

Jude was so lost in his own daydreams that he screamed when somebody leapt out at him from the alleyway. They grabbed his arm and spun him around. When he saw that it was Ashley, he grabbed his stomach and let out a gasp. "You almost gave me a heart attack. I was just coming to see you."

She looked at him with wide eyes, and it was clear she was eager to tell him something. "I was on my way to see you, too. You wouldn't believe the shit that happened last night."

"Your dad?"

"What? No, no. There was some really weird shit that went down though. I found a fucking worm in my sandwich, but then it was gone, like I imagined the whole thing."

"Yeah, well," he said, matching her excitable tone, "I slid into a hot bath and a second later, it was freezing. I mean, it literally went from red-hot to ice-cold in about three seconds. It was impossible, but it happened. And don't even get me started on the two dead kids."

Ashley's eyes widened. For a moment, she stared at him like she didn't know who he was. Then, slowly, her mouth began to move. "Y-You mean, like, two little kids from the olden days? Boy and girl?"

Jude's mouth fell open. "Y-You saw them too? Was it on TV? I thought I was watching *The Hobbit*, but then suddenly I'm watching these two little kids get stabbed to death by their mother. It was the worst thing I've ever seen, Ash."

"I didn't see them get stabbed, but I watched them rot like corpses – maggots in their eyes. I almost puked. Jude, what the hell is going on?"

He shook his head. He'd been hoping she would have the answers. "Maybe it was just some sick movie that was playing. We must have turned to the same channel."

"I was watching Netflix," she said. "It was supposed to be some crappy romantic comedy, not a kiddie snuff film." She put a hand to her neck and sighed, then looked around like she was searching for hidden cameras. Finally, she leaned into Jude and whispered, "It's the woman. This is all because of her. How could the police not find her? She was right there, chained up."

"I wish I had the answer," said Jude. "My mum wants us to change our story so we don't get in trouble, but I don't even know what we would say. If we say we made the whole thing up, we could get into even more trouble."

"I'm not telling anybody that it was a lie. Fuck that. We did nothing except tell the truth. The police must've screwed up somehow. Or..." She shook her head.

Jude tilted his head at her. "What? What is it?"

She let out another sigh. "What if the sicko who chained that woman up came back after we left? What if he saw us? We left her alone, Jude. What if he came and took her someplace else? What if he killed her? Maybe last night was her fucking ghost screwing with us."

"And I thought I was the one with an overactive imagination."

"Yeah, well, that's how messed up all this is."

"One of us should have stayed with her. We did the wrong thing, Ash."

"We were fucking terrified. How were we supposed to know we would run into some abused, naked woman in the woods? If it wasn't for Ricky Dalca, we never would have even been there. Either way, we tried to help her."

It was true – they had tried to help her – but they had also failed. So what should they do now? Did they just move on, change their stories, and hope not to get into too much trouble? Could they put this behind them? Move on like it had never even happened?

Jude grunted, not liking where his thoughts were heading. "We tried to help her," he said, "but we made things worse. I think..." He shook his head and grunted again. "I can't believe I'm saying this, but I think we need to go back into Devil's Ditch. We need to try to find the woman again."

Ashley spluttered. "Are you fucking kidding me? No way am I going back there. The sicko will probably find us and chain us up as well. If he doesn't just kill us."

"That's not going to happen. Either the woman's still out there, and the police missed her somehow, or the sicko got rid of her and covered his tracks. If that's the case, there's no way he would still be hanging around. Either way, we need to go back. If the woman's still there, she still needs our help. If not, well, maybe we can at least find something to prove we're not lying. We're in a bunch of trouble we don't deserve, Ash. Don't you want to do something about it?"

Ashley didn't speak for a moment. She shook her head. Eventually, she said, "I think I'll just accept the trouble, thank you very much."

"Fine, I'll go on my own. After last night's weirdness, we can't just ignore this. You saw those symbols on the floor. You said you pulled a piece of bone from my hand. Something isn't right here, Ash. It's almost supernatural. Maybe the woman was calling out to us last night, pleading for help."

Ashley snickered at him unkindly. "This isn't one of your stupid fantasy books, Jude. Are you trying to say that woman was some kind of ghost?"

"I don't know – really, I don't – but I'm going back to the farmhouse to find some answers. I can't forget about this, Ash, not knowing there's a chance a woman might need our help. But I understand if you don't want to come. You're probably right about it being a bad idea. The problem is, I can't think of a better one."

Jude walked away, but Ashley grabbed him and stopped him. "You're crazy, do you know that? Fuck's sake, this is so dumb."

"You coming or not?"

Ashley sighed. "One down, two down, but you best not get me killed."

"If there are any witches or psychopaths in Devil's Ditch," he said, "then all we have to do is run faster than them. Simple."

"No. All I have to do is run faster than *you*."

The two of them laughed, but they soon fell silent. They barely said a single word as they headed back towards Devil's Ditch.

CHAPTER NINE

Ash still couldn't believe she was doing this. Yesterday had been one of the weirdest, freakiest days of her life. Now she was preparing to do the whole thing over again. To make matters even more bizarre, Jude was the one being brave. She was following him like a lost puppy.

"What do we do if she's still there?" Ashley asked as they cut through the bushes, moving deeper into the woods. "Those chains were right through her hands. We should have brought tools."

Jude glanced over his shoulder at her. "We're not going to do *anything*. I have my phone, so I'll take a picture as proof. Then, one of us can stay behind while the other gets help."

"You want one of us to stay at that creepy farmhouse on our own? Fuck, Jude, I don't know."

"I'll stay," he said. "You can get help."

It was a sunny morning, but things rapidly grew darker as the trees increased in number and their canopies thickened. It was also a little chilly despite the sunshine, and the ground felt damp underfoot. All the same, it was nice to be alone with Jude and away from her parents. They would probably be giving her a lecture right about now if she were at home. When her dad realised she'd snuck out, he was going to blow a fuse.

I'm already grounded. What else can he do to me?

Maybe I don't want to find out.

They reached the part of the woods where Ricky and Lily had chased them yesterday. Ashley traced her index finger along the wound on her cheek and pictured it all over again. The cut had scabbed over. Hopefully, it wouldn't leave a scar. The memory was enough to make her clench her fists. She wanted to punch Lily's freckle-covered face.

I really hate that crazy-haired bitch.

"Okay," Jude said, pointing, "let's cut through here."

They pushed their way through some more bushes. Ashley tried not to snag her clothes. The baggy black T-shirt was one of her favourites. It had no design on it except for the shape of a white hand throwing devil horns. Jude was wearing a T-shirt, too, except it was far more colourful, with white, green and red stripes running in a thin pattern. He looked like an ice cream lolly.

When they reached the top of the slope that led down into Devil's Ditch, they stood beside each other with their hands on their hips, staring towards the bottom. Jude let out a whistle. "Still can't believe we fell all the way down."

"Actually, you pushed me."

"I did it to save you. Pretty heroic if you ask me."

She gave him a light tap on the arm. "The warrior princess is grateful. Now, how are we going to get back down there? I want it to be a lot less painful than last time."

Jude nodded. "I agree. I think the best way to get down is on our stomachs. The more of our bodies touching the ground, the better grip we'll have."

"You've thought about this, huh?"

"A little bit. Just get down on your belly and you'll be fine. I'll go first."

Ashley stood there and watched while Jude got on his knees

and swivelled onto his belly. He scooted backwards over the crest of the slope and flattened himself against the mud. He looked up at her and smiled. "See? It's fine."

With a sigh, Ashley got down beside him, and the two of them shimmied down the slope on their bellies like a pair of demented worms. Once again, she couldn't believe what she was doing. It was absurd. They were searching for a naked woman in the woods.

A woman who might be a ghost or a witch. A woman who might have put a worm in my sandwich last night and screwed with my laptop. Although, why would she do that if she needed help? Couldn't she have asked us in a nice way?

Halfway down the slope, she had to stop and tug at her T-shirt. It had ridden up so high that her bra was exposed. She glanced over at Jude, blushing, but he wasn't looking. In fact, he never looked at her that way. They were like brother and sister. Yet, for a moment, she was embarrassed by the thought of him seeing her underwear.

They reached the bottom of the slope relatively easily, which proved Jude's methods correct. He stood up in front of her with a smug grin on his face. "Easy-peasy," he said.

Ashley pulled at her T-shirt and brushed leaves and twigs off of her. When she realised how muddy she had got, she swore. "Dammit. This is one of my best tops."

"It'll wash clean. Big picture, Ash. Do you remember the way?"

She thought about yesterday's events – remembered looking up at Ricky and Lily from the bottom of the slope – then followed her memory until she recalled which way she and Jude had gone. She pointed. "We went that way."

Jude frowned and looked back and forth. "You sure? I thought we went over there."

Ashley was sure. In fact, she could remember every minute of yesterday with perfect clarity. "We definitely walked that way. Trust me."

"I do." Jude headed in the direction she was pointing. Ashley followed.

They walked for a few minutes, and suddenly the woods seemed unfamiliar. Ashley wondered whether she might have got it wrong. She expected Jude to chide her for getting them lost, but then she spotted something she recognised.

NO TRESPASSING.

Moss and dirt obscured a majority of the sign, but there was no doubt it was the same one they'd seen yesterday. It meant the farmhouse was near.

Ashley found the gap in the bushes where they had pushed through and pulled the branches aside. She waited for Jude to make his way through.

This is his *noble quest. Let* him *be the one to go first.*

Inch by inch, the two of them made their way through the bushes. They reached the clearing on the other side and looked around. Ashley almost expected the farmhouse to be gone, but there it was, just as before, crumbling brick and a missing roof. The weeds and vines still filled every gap, and the entire building was cast in shadow.

Ashley froze in place, unable to move.

What the hell am I doing back here?

Jude was a few steps ahead, but when he realised she wasn't following, he stopped and looked back at her. "It's okay," he said. "We can do this. Everything is going to be fine. One down, two down, right?"

"One down, two down." Ashley took a tentative step forward and got herself moving. She caught up with Jude, and the two of them approached the farmhouse together. The clearing was silent, no birds in the trees and certainly no screaming naked women. There was, however, a dead squirrel – the same one Jude had stepped on yesterday. It was oddly comforting – a confirmation that events had happened as they remembered them.

Jude moved through the clearing until he reached the uneven steps that led inside the farmhouse. He waited for her to join him and then took the first step. Ashley waited for him to go inside and hurried in behind him. As with everything else so far, it was exactly the same as before. The stone-floored room was empty aside from the old fireplace, and the door at the other end was still open as they'd left it. It was hard to see inside the next room without getting closer, but Ashley noticed shadows moving back and forth in the doorway.

Jude wasted no time. He marched forward, hands swinging at his sides. Ashley had never seen him so determined before, yet she also sensed a tension in him. She needed to be ready in case his bravery ran out.

The shadows in the next room continued to move.

Ashley hurried to keep up with Jude. They reached the doorway to the next room and both saw the woman. Both of them gasped. The woman gawked at them, bright green eyes wide and disbelieving.

Wait, weren't her eyes blue?

Jude stammered. "Sh-She's here. I knew it! How did... How did the police not find her?"

Ashley was speechless. She looked into the woman's eyes, and they stared at each other for several moments. Then she looked away and her eyes fell upon something else.

What the fuck?

Dead animals littered the room. Small species, like rats, birds, and squirrels. All of them were torn open, their insides exposed. The smell in the room was unbearable.

"We're here to help you," said Jude. "We're sorry we left you yesterday. You must've been so—"

The woman lunged forward, yanking at her chains, which were still attached through her ankles and hands. The bonds tugged at her flesh and caused the wounds to bleed. She bit at the air, jaws snapping closed over and over. She seemed intent on attacking Jude, hissing at him like she hated him.

"What's wrong with her?" said Jude, backing away. "Why doesn't she understand we want to help her?"

Ashley grabbed him and moved him back into the other room. "I think it's you. You're a man. She's afraid of you. I think... I think I need to stay with her while you go get help."

"I'm not leaving you here, Ash. Something's wrong about all this."

"Yeah, no fucking shit. Look, take a picture of her and get the fuck out of here. Call the police, and this time drag their useless arses here yourself. I want a big fat apology from PC Riaz."

Jude managed a slight chuckle despite the bloodcurdling screams coming from the next room. He glanced back through the doorway at the woman. With a nod, he said, "Okay. You sure you're going to be okay here? There are dead animals everywhere. So many of them... Where did they even—"

Ashley cut him off. "None of this makes sense, so let's not waste time trying to find answers. Just go, all right? Before I chicken out."

Jude pulled his phone out of his pocket and held it sideways to take a snap of the woman. She started yanking on her chains and trying to get free. Like a zombie, her mouth snapped at the air constantly. If not for her vibrant green eyes, she could've been mistaken for a reanimated corpse.

I swear her eyes were blue.

"Hold on," said Jude, fiddling with his phone. "I want one with the flash on."

Ashley waited patiently. Jude's hands shook as he messed with his phone, and he was clearly panicking as he tried to take the picture. Eventually, he got the settings right and took it.

There was a blinding flash.

Ashley gasped and staggered back.

The woman stopped screaming and growled.

Jude looked at Ashley. "What? What's wrong?"

"N-Nothing. Just get going. It's fine. Go."

Jude went to look at his phone to see the picture he had

taken, but when Ashley shouted at him, he put it in his pocket and hurried out of the farmhouse. Then he was gone.

Ashley was alone.

She tried to make sense of what she had seen when the camera had flashed. Her mind could have been playing tricks on her, but if not...

For a split second, almost too fast for her brain to register, she had seen the room change. In the blinding light of the LED flash, the room had altered. The symbol-covered floors had turned to flesh, and the walls wept blood. The woman had changed, too, her hair changing from blonde to brown and her bright green eyes turning as black as oil. There had also been somebody else in the room – a silently screaming man. It had to have been her imagination.

It couldn't have been real.

But would I really imagine something as fucked up as that?

Ashley realised she was shaking. She clenched her fists and tried to get a handle on her fear. She resisted the urge to pee.

"Help me," said a fragile voice.

Ashley turned to face the other room. The woman peered at her with pleading eyes, which were once again green. She was now sobbing and trembling, with snot all over her face. "H-Help me," she said again. "Please."

It was hard to know what was real anymore. Ashley felt lightheaded. This place, this farmhouse, was more than it appeared.

She took a tentative step forward. "Hi. W-What's your name?"

The woman stared at the cracked floor, then back up at Ashley. For a moment, it seemed like she didn't know the answer. "M-My name is Rose. Rose."

Ashley took another step forward, stopping at the edge of the painted triangle on the ground. "Hello, Rose. My name's Ashley. My friend's name is Jude. He's gone to get help. How... How did you end up here, Rose?"

Once again, the woman seemed unsure of the answer. As she trembled, flakes of mud and leaves peeled from her naked body. She clutched at the locket around her neck and swallowed. "I-I don't remember. It's all so... muddy. My mind... It has withered. I beg of you, please do not hurt me further."

"No. No way. Nobody's going to hurt you, Rose. You're going to be okay."

"Will you free me from my bonds? These chains, they bite me so terribly that the pain is now part of me. I do not remember a time without it."

Ashley felt sick. There was so much blood in the room, so many dead animals...

"How long have you been here, Rose?"

"Time long enough to know these four walls intimately. The one who put me here is vile, a wretched abomination. This I know, yet their identity escapes me. Please, take me from this place."

There was something odd about the way Rose spoke. She spoke politely, using words that didn't quite sound right. It was like listening to someone quote Shakespeare. Also, since Jude had left, the woman no longer seemed to be so afraid. She sat calmly on the backs of her heels, almost seeming to smile at Ashley.

"I need to escape this place, Ashley. Please, take me away."

"We just need to wait for help to arrive, okay?"

"You must release me. Liberate me from this bondage."

"I can't. There's no way that I can cut your chains. They're made of..." She went to say steel, but that didn't seem right.

They're more like stone, or...

Bone.

"You need to escape, too," said Rose.

Ashley wasn't sure what she meant, so she shook her head and frowned. "Sorry?"

"You need to escape, Ashley. I am not the only one in need of rescue."

A panic washed over her as she wondered what the woman meant. Was the sicko out here in the woods with them? Was she in danger?

Of course I am.

The sicko must have to come back to the farmhouse regularly to feed the woman and check on her. Maybe that's what Rose was warning her about.

I need to get out of here.

No. I need to wait for Jude to come back with help. That was what we agreed.

Ashley cleared her throat. "I need to escape from what?"

The woman looked at her with an expression of pity. "Your chains."

"What chains?"

"The ones that bind all women. The ones that stifle us and imprison us and force us to obey. You are strong, Ashley, I see that. A strong woman like you deserves to be free. You should fear no man."

The only man in Ashley's life, aside from Jude, who barely counted, was her dad, but it was true she feared him in certain ways. She feared his anger and also his disappointment. She also loved him; loved the man who cuddled her every time she had scraped a knee or got a paper cut. Her dad worked hard to keep her fed and healthy. There was a time when he'd even made her laugh. She feared her dad, sure, but not as much as she loved him.

Ashley shook her head. "I don't know what you're talking about. You're going to be okay, Rose, okay? Just... relax."

The woman lifted her arms, raising the chains that were attached to her bloody palms. "My time to rest is ending. I beg you to release me. Quickly, before my torment begins anew. Take my hands and free me."

"I don't know what you want me to do. Jude has gone to get help. We need to wait. Please, Rose, just... wait with me."

The woman shook her head and sighed. "Trouble comes. You have missed your chance to avoid it."

Ashley didn't reply. Every time she did, the woman said something even more bizarre. She may well have lost the plot.

I think I'm losing the plot too.

Come on, Jude. Please don't be long.

CHAPTER TEN

JUDE MADE it back to Devil's Ditch in less than five minutes, but he stopped at the bottom to catch his breath. Never had he run so fast, and a molten blade was now digging into his ribs. As much as he had wanted to see the woman again, to prove that he wasn't crazy, he was now deeply disturbed. She'd tried to attack him.

She tried to bite me.

It made sense that she would be afraid of him for being a man, if it was indeed a man who had put her in chains, but it still upset him that anybody might see him as a threat. He'd never hurt anybody in his entire life.

Hopefully, the woman would eventually recover enough to learn that he and Ashley had rescued her. It felt wrong to want credit for being a hero, but the thought of it, he had to admit, made him excited. In his fantasies, however, rescuing innocent women had always been a lot less frightening.

He took a few more moments to catch his breath and then surveyed the muddy slope before him. He planned to climb it in the same way he had yesterday – by using a sharp and sturdy stick. It took him several moments, but eventually he found one suitable. Before he started climbing, he pulled out his phone and considered making a call. When he saw he had no signal, the idea went away fast.

He moved to the bottom of the slope and planted the stick a couple of feet up. He heaved himself upwards and repeated the process several times until he was halfway up.

Then he cried out in pain.

A sudden jolt ran through his palm and shocked him, causing him to drop the stick. Before he could reach out and reclaim it, it was already sliding back down the slope.

"Shit!" Jude teetered without support, looking back at an eight-foot fall. He spotted the jagged rock he had only just missed yesterday.

Help me!

He threw himself down on his belly, clinging to the buried roots and pieces of stones that were embedded in the mud. His hand throbbed painfully, and as he lay there on his stomach, he pulled it in front of his face. The bandage his mother had applied came loose, the ends flapping and dirty with mud. Wanting to see what had caused the sudden jolt of pain, he grasped the bandage between his teeth and unravelled it. The fabric was short and soon came free of his hand. Not wanting to reapply the filthy piece of cloth, he let it fall into the mud. Then he turned his hand over to examine his palm.

He screamed and panicked. He nearly fell, and only just got hold of himself in time to keep from tumbling backwards. Forcing himself to breathe, Jude kept his panic at bay. He dug his left hand into the ground and raised his right.

The fat worm wriggled in his wound, thrashing back and forth like it was trying to get free. Blood leaked down his palm and dripped onto his wrist. He felt the worm's every movement, sharp and dagger-like. Unable to let go of the slope, Jude brought his palm to his mouth and bit down on the worm. He yanked his hand away, stretching the worm until it burst free of his wound. The pain was immense, and he feared a pound of flesh had torn loose with the worm, but when he looked, there was only a normal-looking cut. The gash was open and sore, but it looked okay. All the same, Jude spat the worm out and shuddered with revulsion and fear. There was no rational explanation for how a worm had got into his wound.

Jude needed to focus on what was important: getting help for Ashley and the woman. His injuries would have to wait until later.

He continued dragging himself up the slope, but he suddenly slid backwards. Undeterred, he clambered upwards again, digging in his toes and pushing with his legs. Again, he slid backwards. He cried out in frustration, not understanding. The mud beneath him was shifting, liquefying. It was as if the ground itself was trying to keep him from escaping.

An anxious bird took flight in his chest and descended into his stomach. He panted and moaned.

Don't panic, Jude. Do not panic.

I can do this.

The trusted mage will not give up. The warrior princess is relying on him.

With a defiant shout, Jude dug both hands into the mud and ignored the pain in his injured palm. He pushed with both feet, launching himself upwards. Before the mud had time to fight him, he dug his hands in again and launched himself a second time. With everything he had left, he scrambled up the slope.

The slope became a vertical swamp, as much liquid as it was solid. It gave off a stink, something awful, and it felt like Jude was wading through shit. He did not give up, propelling himself forward.

He slid backwards.

No. I'm getting out of here.

He threw himself upwards one last time, his hands sinking into the wet mud. He planted his feet flat against the slope and took a risk – he stood up straight. Gravity tried to pull him backwards, but before it had a chance, he threw himself toward the top of the slope. He landed painfully on hard, flat ground.

He rolled onto his back, panting and laughing.

He had succeeded.

The noble mage's quest continues.

He spent the next couple of minutes on his back, knowing he had to get going again but needing to catch his breath first. Climbing the muddy hill had taken everything out of him, and he was absolutely caked in rancid mud. His stomach gurgled and begged him to puke. His legs were numb. Yet he felt energised and alive too.

He got back to his feet and continued on. It wouldn't take long to get back to the footpath. Then he could race home and have his mum call the police. This time, PC Riaz would have no option except to believe him. Like Ashley, he wanted an apology.

I want to be a hero.

As he moved through the woods, it was as if the very trees were trying to impede him. Maybe it was his numb legs making him clumsy, but he tripped and stumbled every few feet and scratched himself on nearly every bush. Once or twice he had to double back and find an alternative route as the way ahead became impassable. It took a while for him to make it to the edge of the woods, but through the final swaths of bushes, he spotted the footpath.

He stepped into the shallow ditch and prepared to run the rest of the way home. He had just taken his first step when something collided with him. Unable to keep from falling, he tripped over his feet and collapsed into the ditch. A pitiful cry escaped his lips as his wounded palm came down on a pile of sharp twigs.

Before he knew what was happening, he was being dragged back to his feet by unkind hands. Ricky Dalca glared at him. "We've been looking for you, Judy. Where's flabby tits? You two never go nowhere without each other."

"Sh-She's in the woods. Devil's Ditch. I'm going to get help."

Lily stood behind Ricky. He turned to her and exchanged a confused look. When he turned back to Jude, he was frowning.

"What are you talking about? Help for what? Why are you covered in so much fucking mud?"

Jude tried to pull away, but Ricky had both hands clenched around his T-shirt. He had no choice but to answer the question. "She... I... We need to call the police, Ricky."

"Fuck that," said Lily. "What the hell do you need the police for?"

Maybe to arrest you two psychopaths.

What do I tell them?

It would be good to share the burden of what he knew, but there was always a chance they wouldn't believe him and beat him up anyway. There was also the possibility that they *would* believe him and beat him up. It was hard to tell with Ricky and Lily. "We-We-We found a w-woman in the w-w-woods. She needs help. Please, just let me go."

For a moment, both Ricky and Lily were silent. Then, in unison, they both let out a laugh.

Lily sucked her teeth and stamped her foot like it was hilarious. "Judy has proper gone and lost it now, mate. Woman in the woods? What the fuck?"

"I'm telling the truth. She's chained up in an old farmhouse."

Ricky frowned, no longer laughing. "There ain't no houses in these woods, you freak. There ain't jack shit."

"He's talking bollocks," said Lily. "He's just trying to avoid getting a good beating."

Jude tried to pull away again, but it was still impossible to get free. He grunted, then sighed in defeat. "Look, you guys, I'm telling the truth. Once the police get involved, they're not gunna be happy hearing how you stopped me from getting help for somebody who needs it."

A fist struck Jude right in the centre of his torso and sent the air wailing from his lungs. He doubled over, groaning in misery, but Ricky forced him to stand back up straight. "I don't talk to the fucking police, you little wanker. You get the pigs onto me and I'll stamp on your skull and leave you a vegetable. D'you get me?"

Jude couldn't breathe, let alone speak, so he just nodded repeatedly. Now, more than ever, he wanted to run home. He was tired of being hurt and afraid and weak. He wanted his mum.

"Hey! What are you kids up to?"

Lily swore. "Fuck! Someone's coming. Get him into the woods, Ricky."

Ricky frowned. "What?"

"Get him in the woods, innit? I want to see what him and his girlfriend are up to in there."

Jude searched for the passer-by who had attempted to intervene. It was an old man walking a dog, but he was thirty metres away at least. When Ricky and Lily started dragging him across the ditch and into the woods, he knew there wasn't going to be any rescue. Even if the passer-by wanted to help, he was too old. He would never catch up with them in the woods.

Jude tried one last time to struggle free, but Ricky punched him in the small of the back and took the fight right out of him. "Forget it, Judy," he said. "You ain't going anywhere." He bent Jude's arm behind his back and marched him forward. "Let's go see this woman. And if you're lying, I'm going to bury you out here, understand?"

Jude nodded and held back tears.

CHAPTER ELEVEN

Rose didn't stop talking. She continued spouting gibberish, mixed in with the odd moment of sense. What Ashley didn't like at all, however, was how the woman kept acting as if she knew all about her life. She kept going on about how Ashley was being held down and silenced, and that there was an entire world waiting for her if she just seized her power as a woman and took what she wanted. Although she could have been saying it about anyone, Rose's words somehow resonated with Ashley. She *did* feel powerless.

Powerless and angry.

Ashley edged towards the open doorway. "I... I think I might just check outside and see if anybody's coming." The truth was she needed some fresh air. The stink of the dead animals – and Rose herself – was making her nauseous. She also couldn't take anymore of the woman's babbling.

Her madness is gunna drive me insane.

Rose yanked on her chains but showed no discomfort as they tugged at her wounds and made the exposed bones in her hands visibly flex. "Stay! Release me so that you and I may leave here. Do not allow me to be rescued by so-called good men. There are no good men in this world, Ashley."

"I've already told you, I can't free you. Somebody will be here soon. Jude will be back. Just... be patient."

Even though the woman protested, Ashley left Rose alone in the strange symbol-covered room. It felt wrong, but at least she wasn't running away like last time. She just needed some air.

I'm not going anywhere. I'm not leaving her.

I just can't be right next to her.

Outside, the clearing had grown dull. Beyond the thick canopy of trees, the sun had retreated behind the clouds. With a shudder, she looked around, eyeing the thick bushes and broad tree trunks.

The sicko could be hiding anywhere.

He could be watching me right now. If Jude doesn't get back soon with help, he might find me lying dead beside Rose.

Please hurry up, Jude.

The stench from inside the farmhouse followed her outside, and even when she stepped away from the building, her nausea continued. She spotted the dead squirrel lying on the ground and grimaced at the maggots and worms feasting on its corpse. Then she spotted something similar nearby – another dead animal – but larger. A flash of white in the corpse's bloody grey fur told her it might have once been a badger. She'd never seen one before, but apparently they were dangerous. Like the squirrel, the badger's rotting remains were riddled with maggots and worms. She could almost hear them squirming.

Ashley yelped as something in the nearby trees moved. She glanced to her left and saw the bushes shaking. Her immediate thought was that the sicko was coming to get her, but when she realised it was Jude, she put her hands on her knees and doubled over. "Fuck, it's you! Did you find any—"

Ricky and Lily appeared, shoving Jude and marching him through the gap between the bushes.

Ashley groaned and instinctively took a step back.

What the hell are they doing here?

"What the fuck is going on, Jude? Are you okay?"

Jude didn't look happy. He was covered in mud, and from the way Ricky was wrenching his arm behind his back, it was clear he hadn't brought the two bullies back with him willingly. When Jude turned towards Ashley, he looked utterly defeated. He mouthed the word '*sorry*'.

She tried to smile to let him know it was okay, but she couldn't manage it. Instead of help, he had brought the exact opposite. "Jude, did you call the police?"

"No one is calling the police," said Lily. She broke away from Ricky and marched towards Ashley. "D'you get me, slag?"

Ashley clenched her fists. "This has nothing to do with you, Lily, so fuck off. We need to call the police. There's a—"

"A woman, yeah. Judy told us all about it. So come on, where is she? Inside that house?" Lily looked over at the farmhouse and put her hands on her hips. "Can't believe this place is out here in the middle of the woods. Wonder if there's anything worth stealing."

"Why are you even here, Lily?" Ashley snarled. "You usually hang around the shops, so why are you here messing with us?"

She shrugged. "Got caught robbing, innit. Lying low for a while. Think we might be hanging around the playground for a while, so sure we'll be seeing a lot of each other." She started towards the farmhouse.

Jude called out from where Ricky was still restraining him at the edge of the clearing. "Don't go in there. The woman inside is afraid. She needs help."

"Shut it!" Ricky shoved Jude in the back and sent him stumbling forward. He quickly regained his balance and rushed over to Ashley's side. She put a hand on his arm and squeezed.

Lily walked towards the farmhouse, but Ashley hurried to block her. "Don't!"

"Get the fuck out of my way."

"You can't go in there. The woman's name is Rose, and she's in a bad way. Jude was going to call the police to get some help."

Jude looked at Ashley. "You know her name? Did she speak to you?"

"A bit."

Lily looked back at Ricky. "You believe this shit?"

Ricky shrugged. He actually seemed a little unnerved by the situation. Whatever had happened out in the woods between him and Jude, he probably hadn't actually believed that there was an old farmhouse out here. "Maybe we should bounce," he said. "If the pigs are gunna end up getting involved, I don't wanna be."

Lily rolled her eyes. "Don't you want to know if these two freaks are telling the truth? If they are, there's a naked fuck toy in that house, and I want to see her for myself. Come on, Ricky, let's just go take a quick look."

Ricky nodded. "I suppose we can take a quick look. If there *is* a woman in there, though, we should get the fuck out of here. Let Judy and flabby tits deal with the headache."

"You're not going in there," said Ashley, refusing to move out of Lily's way.

Lily expelled a gust of air from her nostrils like a snorting bull. She glanced back at Ricky again, a slight smirk on her pale, freckle-covered face. Then she threw a punch that struck Ashley right in the side of the head and sent her stumbling to the ground. She came down right on top of the dead badger and yelled in horror and disgust. She rolled away into the grass and frantically wiped her hands on her T-shirt.

Jude tried to help her, but Ricky reached out and grabbed the back of his T-shirt. The two of them did a dance, Jude trying to break free and Ricky fighting to hold on to him. Eventually, Jude escaped and made it over to Ashley.

Her head was spinning, and when she tried to get up, her legs folded and she fell back down. Lily had really given her a wallop. Jude got down in the grass beside her and put an arm around her. "Are you okay?"

"That... That bitch. I'm going to fucking kill her."

Lily pulled out her knife and pressed the release. The blade slid out with an audible *snick!* "Still has your blood on it," she purred. "Stay down or I'll let it drink some more. Come on, Ricky, let's have a mooch inside this house."

Ricky sniggered, but there was a slight nervousness in his eyes. He kept glancing around at the bushes, and when he made eye contact with Ashley, he almost appeared sorry. It didn't stop him catching up to Lily, though.

Ashley rubbed the side of her jaw and moaned while she and Jude sat in the grass. "I hope they break their necks in there," she said.

Jude nodded. "I tried to get help, Ash, I swear. I was nearly home, but I ran straight into the two of them. I'm sorry."

Ashley grabbed the back of his messy brown hair and pulled their foreheads together. "This isn't your fault, Jude. The world is full of fucking arseholes, but you're not one of them. We'll get help, I promise."

"So long as Ricky and Lily don't kill us and leave our bodies in this clearing."

"Not happening." Ashley got up, testing her legs to make sure they were once again obeying her brain. Jude stood up beside her, keeping a hand on her back. She looked at him, dismayed by the state of him but also annoyed that he let these things happen. Why didn't he ever defend himself? Why did she always have to be the one to stand up to Ricky and Lily, or whatever bullshit they were dealing with that day? "We have to go back inside, Jude. Lily's a goddamn psycho. There's no telling what she'll do. We need to protect Rose."

Jude frowned. "They're just going to look around. What's the worst they can do?"

"With those two, who knows? We can't leave Rose alone with them, but I can't stand up to them by myself. I need you to have my back, Jude. One down, two down, right?"

"I don't think I can…" Jude didn't finish what he was saying. He nodded. "One down, two down."

Ashley started towards the farmhouse. Jude followed. No sound came from inside the building, and the exposed roof timbers cast angular shadows across the clearing. No part of the place was welcoming. Ashley glanced at Jude before she went up the steps, making sure he was still with her. He had turned pale beneath his muddy mask, and he was trembling slightly, but he gave her a nod to show he had her back. So long as he didn't panic, she trusted him.

Ricky was standing in the farmhouse's front room, staring at the fireplace. When he saw Jude and Ashley enter, he flinched. His expression was grim, and even in the shadowy interior it was clear he'd lost some of his colour. He shook his head at them and said, "You two weren't lying. Who the hell did that to her? They put... they put the chains right through her hands."

Ashley didn't answer. She looked past Ricky and into the next room. Through the open doorway, she saw Lily standing with her hands on her hips while Rose knelt inside the triangle a few feet away. Rose seemed to be muttering something, but it was unclear what. The smell inside the farmhouse was rotten. Jude covered his nose, but Ashley breathed the odour in. She'd spent so much time doubting herself in the last twenty-four hours, and she didn't want to dull a single sense. This situation was real. What she was seeing and smelling was real.

But something about the situation felt off.

Why wasn't Rose screaming? Whenever Jude and Ashley had interacted with her, she'd been like a wild animal, and had only calmed down when she'd been alone with Ashley. Now there were four people in the farmhouse and she was totally calm.

What is she muttering to Lily?

Lily turned around to face the front room, and for a moment she almost seemed surprised to see them all standing there. "The fuck have you two been doing in here?" she said. "You're sick. This is some messed-up shit."

"We didn't do this," Jude protested. "We found her like this."

"What are you talking about? There's no one here. You're both full of shit." Lily looked back into the other room and shook her head, making a sound of disgust. "All of these dead animals... You two need locking up. This is serial killer shit."

Ashley stepped forward. "What are you doing, Lily? Rose is right there in front of you, so stop screwing around."

Rose remained on her knees, sitting calmly and looking up at Lily, who was about three feet away from her, just outside the triangle. She was still mumbling something, but it was still too quiet to make out. Every now and then, she lifted her hands and rattled her chains.

Ricky moved away from the fireplace. He still looked ill, and his glances around the room were furtive, like he didn't want to focus on any one thing for too long, but he stood up straight as he spoke. "Lily? What are you playing at? They were telling the truth. We need to help this woman. Look at the state of her."

Lily scrunched up her face, making her ugly face even less pleasant. She still had her flick knife, but it was hanging loosely by her side. "There's nothing in this room except a bunch of dead animals. Are you all fucking crazy?" She put her forearm under her nose. "Fuck, it stinks in here. Ricky, sort your head out before I give you a slap."

Ashley stared at Jude, but he seemed as confused as she was. She took a step towards Lily, trying to understand how the other girl could appear so genuine about something so obviously false. "Do you really not see her, Lily? She's right there. Just... look!"

For once, Lily did as she was told. She turned around and stepped into the room, only an inch away from the edge of the painted triangle. She didn't see Rose at all. In fact, she reacted only to the dead animals littering the room.

"Do you see the symbols?" Jude asked from the other room. "On the floor."

Lily glanced back through the doorway at him. She was clearly confused, but she overrode it with aggression. "What fucking symbols? Seriously, what the hell is this?"

Ricky ran both hands through his short, spiky hair. "This is messed up, yo. Lily, let's just go."

Lily glared at him suspiciously. "Ricky? Why are you acting weird? Do you really see something? You believe these freaks? There's a woman in this room?"

Ricky shrugged and attempted a chuckle, but it sounded false. "Nah, I don't believe shit. It just stinks in here, innit? I wanna get out of here so we can spark up a joint."

Lily continued glaring, but something seemed to gradually dawn on her. "You do see something, don't you? You're as crazy as these two, mate."

"I just wanna go, Lil."

Ashley moved towards Lily, putting her hands up to show that she didn't want a fight. "It doesn't matter if you believe us or not, Lily. Just get out of here."

Lily stepped out of the room and approached Ashley. "You don't tell me what to do, slag." She pulled out her knife, waving it back and forth in front of her face. "You want me to fucking cut you again?"

Ashley felt her anger rise merely from looking at Lily's face. She wanted to reach out and shove her thumbs into the girl's eyes and pop them like gooey zits. But, despite the rage building up inside of her, Ashley kept quiet. She just wanted Lily to go. A fight wasn't going to help anyone.

"I asked you a question, slag. Do you want me to cut you again?"

Ashley felt her heart beat faster. "No, I just want you to go."

Lily smirked. She put the knife down by her side and shrugged. "Okay, I'll go."

In the corner of Ashley's eye, Ricky and Jude let out relieved sighs.

Lily made a move as though she was about to walk away, but then she stopped and smirked right in Ashley's face. "Get down on your knees and kiss my feet."

Ashley swallowed. "What?"

Lily glanced down at her trainers, then back up at Ashley. "Get down on your knees, kiss my feet, and I'll leave you alone. Or..." She raised the knife and held it between them. "I'll slice your ugly fucking face again, and this time I'll leave a scar, I promise."

Ricky moved away from the fireplace. "Come on, Lily. It isn't worth it."

"Shut the fuck up, Ricky. You're acting like a pussy and you're pissing me off."

Ricky folded his arms and backed off. He began tapping his foot nervously and didn't seem at all like the tough guy he usually appeared to be. Lily, however, was committed to being a monster. She glared at Ashley, waiting for an answer.

"I'm not kissing your feet, Lily. Just go."

"Knife it is then." Lily grabbed the back of Ashley's head and pressed the knife against her cheek.

The leash broke on Ashley's anger. She swung an arm and clobbered Lily around the side of the head. "Here's your receipt, bitch!"

Lily staggered backwards, taken by surprise. The punch had landed well, but it didn't knock her down. Ashley's hand was throbbing. She shook it and spat a stream of curse words.

Lily launched herself forward and headbutted Ashley right in the middle of the nose. As quickly as the fight had started, it ended, as blood gushed from her face and she suddenly found herself blinded by her own tears. She could only just make out the blurry shape of Lily standing in front of her.

"Now I'm going to make a real mess of your face. Hold still, bitch."

"Leave her the fuck alone!"

Ashley wiped away her tears in time to see Jude launch himself across the room and tackle Lily. Perhaps it was asking too much to expect him to throw a punch, but it was still surprising to witness him show any kind of aggression. With both hands, he shoved Lily hard in the chest. She flew backwards, staggering on her heels, and toppled right through the doorway and into the next room.

Rose scooted aside to avoid being landed on. Lily crashed against the stone floor, right in the centre of the painted triangle.

Ricky, Ashley, and Jude stood in the other room, frozen. Nobody spoke. They all watched silently as Lily lay on her side in a pained heap. "Fuck!" she said in a moan and clutching her elbow. "You're going to pay for that. Believe me, you are going to fucking pay for that." She pushed herself up into a sitting position and pointed a finger. "Grab the little fucker, Ricky."

But Ricky didn't move. He stared at Rose, who had risen to her feet as Lily rose to hers. It was now abundantly obvious that Lily really didn't see the woman. She showed zero recognition of there being anybody in the room except for her. It made no sense.

Why can't she see Rose when the rest of us can?

Lily glared at Ricky. "I said, grab him. What the hell is wrong with—"

Rose moved like somebody had pressed the fast-forward button on reality. One instant, she was standing beside Lily, completely unmoving; the next, she was standing behind her, mouth open wide and screaming. She moved again in a blink, yanking at her chains until the fragile bones in her hands shattered and the flesh of her palms split apart. Then, like a ravenous tiger, she bit into Lily's neck with brown, rotting teeth.

CHAPTER TWELVE

Lily's eyes stretched wide a half-second before her mouth did, then she was wailing at the top of her lungs. She made a screeching sound Jude likened to a motorway pileup, and she slashed the air with the knife which she'd somehow kept hold of. Rose moved in sync with her victim, continuing to bite into Lily's pale flesh as she tried to get away. Blood spurted into her pale, freckled face.

"Lily!" Ricky broke free of his fear and raced to help his friend. Without hesitation, he launched himself into the next room and grabbed Lily's desperately grasping hands. He pulled her away from Rose, but the woman didn't give her up willingly. Her teeth tore away a massive chunk of Lily's neck, opening up a gigantic, bloody hole beneath her jaw. Lily's knees failed her, and Rose embraced her as she slumped to the ground.

Lily gasped in horror as she finally saw Rose.

She reached out a hand again to Ricky and tried to push Rose away with the other. Her fingers tangled in Rose's necklace and the locket broke free.

Lily went limp. Her eyes fluttered halfway between dead and alive.

With a roar of effort, Ricky heaved on Lily's outstretched arm with both hands and tried to pull her towards the open doorway. He sobbed and wailed, determined to get his friend out of there, but Rose held her in place inside the triangle, seemingly without effort. She glared at Ricky, chuckling quietly to herself, then bit into Lily again, this time on her stomach. Lily was barely conscious, but she shuddered in pain as great torrents of blood gushed from her neck and abdomen. Her eyes glazed over like she was dreaming with them open. She blew bubbles between her bloodstained lips. Ricky still had his hands wrapped around her arm, but slowly his blood-slicked fingers slipped and lost their grip.

Rose dragged Lily's body into the centre of the room, guarding her prize like a cat with a mouse.

The whole time, Jude stood and watched in utter horror. Everyone was there because of him. He had decided to come back to the farmhouse, imagining himself as a hero, but instead he had got Lily killed.

What have I done?

Knowing they needed to get the hell out of there, he leapt forward and grabbed Ricky around the waist. He was in shock too, watching in silence while Rose chewed on his best friend like a slab of steak. "Ricky, we have to go."

Ricky fought Jude away. "No, I have to help her." He started to move. *"I need to—"*

"Stop!" Ashley shouted. She was standing in the other room and threw up an arm. "Ricky, don't step inside the triangle. That's what Lily did and she... Just... get back."

Ricky stopped and froze. He peered down at his feet and took a step backwards. His trainer had been only two inches from the triangle's brownish outline. Rose stopped her feasting and smiled at him with a mouth dripping blood. "You have something of mine, boy."

Jude grabbed Ricky around the waist again. This time there was no fighting. Both hurried into the other room to join Ashley.

"We need to get the fuck out of here," said Ashley. "Right now."

"D'ya think?" said Jude. He took one last look at the carnage in the other room. Then the three of them sprinted out of the farmhouse and raced across the clearing.

Ricky was sobbing.

Ashley swore repeatedly, a sure sign that she was okay.

They reached the bushes and stopped to catch their breath, looking at each other and panting. Jude couldn't bear the silence, so he spoke. "You were right, Ashley. Rose can't leave the triangle. It's some sort of trap to hold her in place."

Ashley nodded. "The farmhouse is a fucking prison."

Ricky shook his head, staring blindly at the trees ahead of them. "She tore Lily apart. She... she was eating her like an animal."

"Lily couldn't see Rose," said Ashley. "That's why she wandered inside the triangle. It makes no sense; why couldn't she see her?"

There was a bloodcurdling scream from the house.

"Don't worry," said Jude, hands shaking at his sides. "She can't leave the triangle. We're safe."

Providing a punchline to a horrifyingly grim joke, Rose appeared in the farmhouse's doorway. She descended the crooked stone steps and peered in their direction. Lily's blood covered her naked body. Her blonde hair had turned jet black, as had a wiry patch between her legs.

His theory about Rose being trapped in the triangle was clearly incorrect.

The three of them screamed in terror and fought one another to get through the gap in the bushes. Jude let them go first. He dared to look back one last time at the monster he had let out of its cage.

What the hell is she?

A demon?

A witch?

Rose lifted a ruined hand into the air and, with a smile, she waved at Jude.

Jude hurried into the gap, another scream escaping his lips.

CHAPTER THIRTEEN

THEY CLIMBED Devil's Ditch without stopping to plant sticks in the ground. The three of them were so terrified they scrambled up the muddy slope on their bellies, clawing and digging with everything they had. Halfway up, Ashley tore off part of a thumbnail and growled in agony, but her fear kept her climbing until she reached the top.

Jude completed the ascent a full minute slower than she did, but she waited for him. No way was she going to leave him behind. She patted him on the back as he climbed to his feet. "You good?"

Jude clutched his wounded hand against his chest. It was bleeding badly and was probably what had delayed him. "Yeah... I'm fine. Let's not stop."

"Wait!" Ricky had slid a few feet down the slope and was frantically trying to claw his way back up. "Don't go without me. Please!"

Ashley looked at Jude and shrugged. "Fuck him."

She turned to leave, but Jude crouched at the edge of the slope.

Ashley rolled her eyes and waited. Only Jude could stop to

help the same arsehole who had been tormenting him for the last three years. In fact, this whole nightmare had started with Ricky punching Jude in the stomach on the overpass.

Jude's a better person than I am. I don't forgive so easily.

Jude reached out a hand and helped Ricky up onto the flat ground. The bully was a trembling mess, and he clung to Jude like a life jacket. "Shit! I thought you were going to leave me."

"We should have," said Ashley, sneering.

Ricky actually nodded in agreement. "Maybe."

The three of them took off into the woods, Ricky taking the lead now it was once again a flat race. They each knew where they were going, so they dodged the trees and bushes in unison and exited the woods at the same time. Jude lost his footing in the shallow ditch and tripped. Doing something Ashley could barely believe, Ricky stopped to help him back to his feet.

They were finally on the footpath, the woods behind them.

No one was around, despite the perfect dog-walking weather. The sun was unobstructed now that they were out from beneath the tree canopy. The sky was cloudy but mostly blue. It felt like there should have been people jogging and taking strolls, but the footpath was deserted. Part of Ashley irrationally feared that the world had disappeared in her absence and that they were the only people left on Earth. Once again, she doubted her own sanity.

What the hell happened at that farmhouse?

Is Lily really dead?

Rose. Who the hell is she?

What the hell is she?

Ricky looked around nervously. "Where do we go now?"

Ashley snapped out of her paranoia and shrugged. "To get help."

"We'll go to my house," said Jude. "My mum will listen to us. Maybe."

They were all out of breath, so rather than run, they power-walked until they reached the playground. There, they found the twins. The brothers were sitting on the swings, and they were clearly confused when they spotted Ricky with Jude and Ashley. One of them – Ashley thought Tommy – stood up and came over to the playground's railing. He leant over the bar and pulled a face. "Ricky, what you doin' with these two?"

Ricky stammered, and when he failed to find words, he shrugged.

Tommy raised an eyebrow, then nodded at Jude. "The fuck happened to your hand, man?"

Jude looked down at his bloodstained hand and fumbled for an answer. "Glass on the playing fields."

"That sucks, man. Little kids play there."

Danny came over to join his brother at the railing. He looked at Ricky. "Hey, where's Lil? She texted earlier saying she was wid you."

Ricky swallowed and didn't do a good job of acting unsuspiciously. "Sh-She, um, pissed off about an hour ago, blud. Think she went to see her brother."

Danny nodded, but his eyes narrowed. "A'ight. We're heading down the newsagent to get some Rizla. You down?"

Ashley expected Ricky to say no, seeing as they had a murder to report, but he surprised her by saying, "Yeah, I'm down. I need to buy some too, innit?"

Jude grabbed hold of Ricky's wrist and protested. "We need you to come to my house."

Ricky shoved him aside. "Fuck off, Judy. We ain't friends."

Jude stared at him, clearly trying to convey a message. Ashley nudged Jude and told him not to waste his time. "Like I said earlier. Fuck him."

Ricky moved to join the twins, clearly willing to delude himself that everything was normal.

"Hey, Ricky," said Tommy, still hanging over the railing. He held up a rolled cigarette. "You got a light, blud?"

"Yeah, man. Hold on." Ricky stopped and reached into his pocket. He pulled out a clear plastic lighter, but something else fell out onto the ground. Ashley was close enough to see what it was.

Rose's locket.

Ricky froze, staring down at it like a lit bomb. His mouth worked silently for a few seconds as he tried to form words. "I... I grabbed it from her. I-It was in her hand when I tried to... I forgot I had it. I put it in my pocket when we climbed the slope."

Behind the railing, Danny frowned. "The fuck you on about, Ricky? What is that? Jewellery? Whose is it?"

"It's mine," said Ashley. She marched over and grabbed the locket off the ground. To sell the lie a little more, she glared at Ricky like he'd stolen it from her. It wasn't hard because she hated the sonofabitch, but she was also doing it to protect him. "Can't believe you took this, you prick. It was my grandmother's."

Ricky got a hold of himself and seemed to realise she was playing a part for his benefit. He shrugged his shoulders and rolled his eyes as if she were a lump of shit on his shoe. "Whatever, bitch. Get out of my sight before I spark you out."

Ashley shook her head in disgust, turned on the toes of her trainers, and rejoined Jude, who was standing a little further back. The two of them left, shoulder to shoulder, with their heads turned so that they could speak quietly.

"We need him to come with us," Jude whispered. "The police will want to talk to him. He needs to back us up."

"I'm not sure that's a good idea," said Ashley. "I mean, what the hell do we even say? You really want to tell the police that a crazy, naked witch in the woods tore Lily Barnes to shreds – a girl we just so happen to hate. I don't even want to imagine what her crazy family might do if they hear we were with Lily when she..." She shook her head and hissed. "Look, Ricky clearly wants to pretend like this the whole thing didn't happen, so perhaps we should do the same."

Jude's eyes went wide. "We can't ignore this, Ash. That woman – Rose – is still out there in the woods. What if she hurts someone else? What if she hurts us?"

"I just... I just need to think. There are no options that feel like they're going to go well for us. Why the hell did we go back there, Jude? We're so stupid."

"It was because I made us. Ash, I'm so sorry."

She put a hand up, not wanting him to feel any sorrier for himself than he already did. "You could never have known. At least we're alive, which is more than I can say for Lily. Do you..."

"Do I *what*?"

"Feel bad for her? I'm not sure that I do. Does that make me evil?"

Jude clutched his wounded hand against his stomach. Once the pain stopped, he looked at her. "You're not evil, Ash. Lily didn't deserve what happened to her – nobody would deserve that – but she was a bad person. Not just mixed up, but an actual rotten person that was probably never going to be anything else. Even Ricky's better than her. I almost feel like it's a front with him."

Ashley had got the same impression briefly when Ricky had helped Jude up from the shallow ditch, but then, as soon as he had seen the twins, he'd gone right back to being an arsehole. All the same, she'd had his back when he had dropped the locket on the floor. He was in this with them, and they all needed to stick together.

She lifted the locket now and examined it. It was chunky and round, possibly gold or something similar. Dull rather than shiny and dotted with tiny green flecks, it had a clasp on the side to open it. She prized it apart slowly, fearing it might explode in a puff of poisonous gas. But all she found inside was a pair of tiny photographs.

Her breath hitched in her throat, and she almost dropped the locket. "It... It's them. It's the children."

Jude squinted and looked closer at the locket. He exhaled

loudly and began nodding. "It's the same kids I saw on TV. The two kids I watched get stabbed."

"I saw them too. Rotting in the ground. Jude, who are they?"

"They must be Rose's kids. Why else would she have their photographs around her neck? Shit, she's going to want this back, isn't she?"

"I don't know. Maybe we should call the police." She put a hand to her face and groaned. "But we still have no idea what to say. No, we shouldn't speak to anybody until we have a story somebody is going to believe. This isn't just a woman in the woods anymore. Lily's dead. That's murder – and the police aren't going to go searching for some naked witch in the woods. They'll pin it on somebody else."

Jude blubbered like he was about to sob. Fortunately, he didn't. "Y-You mean somebody like us? You reckon we could get the blame for this?"

"I just think... I think maybe we say nothing for now. Let's see how things play out."

Jude didn't reply, and the two of them fell into silence. Ashley slipped the locket back in her jeans pocket and thought about the two children. When she'd seen them on her laptop, it had looked like years ago. Their clothes were old-fashioned. If the children belonged to Rose, then how old would that make her? It made no sense.

She can't be their mother.

They walked the rest of the way without exchanging a word. When they reached Jude's front door, they stopped to look at each other. "We're really not going to call the police?" he said. "Lily's family will be worried."

"Lily's family are psychopaths, and she's gone whether we say anything or not, so let's just think about us, okay?"

Jude nodded and opened the front door.

His mother was standing in the hallway, talking with somebody.

PC Riaz turned to face them. "Ah, just the two people I've come to see."

CHAPTER FOURTEEN

Jude almost fell. The shock of seeing PC Riaz standing in the hallway sent a shockwave straight along his thighs. He had to grab hold of the stairway banister to keep himself upright. Ashley came up behind him and put a hand on his back.

PC Riaz raised an eyebrow. "Are you kids okay? Looks like you've seen a ghost."

Jude's mind was blank, which was why he was glad when Ashley answered.

"You startled us, that's all. Is everything okay?"

His mum chuckled. "Of course, honey. The officer just wants to go over your story one last time."

"Well," said PC Riaz, "I'll decide if everything's okay after I hear what you kids have to say for yourselves. Why don't we take a seat in the kitchen?"

"I'll put the kettle on," his mum said. "It's almost lunchtime. Can I make you a sandwich?"

"Not for me, thank you, Ms Gowdie."

Ashley followed PC Riaz into the kitchen while Jude remained in the hallway and took a deep breath. The plan was to keep quiet about what had happened today, but what did they say about yesterday? Did they recant their story and say they were lying all along? Lying to the police felt like a bad idea, even when the truth was awful.

His mum called out from the kitchen. He realised he was dawdling. "Sweetheart? Are you coming?"

Jude went into the kitchen and sat beside Ashley while his mum stood in the corner watching the kettle boil. Her hands were placed flat on the counter and she was tapping her fingers. PC Riaz sat completely still and said nothing. He just stared at Jude and Ashley.

Eventually, Ashley broke the silence. "I'm sorry about yesterday. I think... I think Jude and I must've got spooked or something. We went into that old farmhouse, and it was so dark. I thought I saw a woman, but it was probably an animal. I screamed and started running, and I didn't stick around long enough to make sure. Jude only panicked because I was panicking. Honestly, I didn't mean to cause any trouble. What would be the point? I thought there was a woman who needed help, but I was wrong."

Jude glanced at her, slightly surprised by the words gushing out of her mouth.

PC Riaz remained silent. After a moment, he turned to face Jude. "Is that correct, Jude? Was this all a case of too much excitement?"

Jude swallowed and felt like he was sweating. The officer's stare was intense. "I-I suppose so."

"Well, did you see a woman in that farmhouse or not?"

"I... I..."

PC Riaz leant forward, his stare increasing its intensity. "Jude, I need you to be very honest with me right now. Did you see a woman in that farmhouse or did your imagination get the better of you?"

Jude flinched as something struck his shin beneath the table. In the corner of his eye, he saw Ashley glaring at him. He knew what he needed to say, but it was like standing on a cliff edge. If he took a step forward, he would fall, with no way of stopping himself if he changed his mind. As soon as he said there was no woman in the farmhouse, he would be a liar. He couldn't take that back.

I will be lying to the police.

Can I really do that? Isn't the truth the best option, no matter the situation? I would rather get caught telling the truth than telling a lie.

But if I lie now, everything might work out okay. It could be over.

I don't think this will be over.

"I..."

"Kettle's boiled," his mum said, and she moved over to PC Riaz with a big smile on her face. "What can I get you, Officer?"

PC Riaz sat back in his chair and folded his arms. "Nothing for me, thank you."

Ashley kicked Jude beneath the table again. He looked at her, and she mouthed something that he didn't catch. Her meaning, however, was obvious: don't say anything about the woman.

PC Riaz leant forward again and resumed his intense stare. A shiver ran up Jude's spine. He wriggled in his chair. "I suppose, maybe, you know—"

"Jude, I want a straight answer, please."

"Well... It's just that—"

Ashley beat a fist on the table. "Dammit, Jude, just say it. Say we were wrong about the whole thing and that we're idiots. There was no woman. Say it!"

PC Riaz put a hand up to stop Ashley. "Quiet! I want to hear Jude answer for himself. I want to know—"

Jude could hold it in no longer. "There was a woman! There was a woman chained up in that farmhouse and she's crazy. She killed Lily Barnes. She ripped her apart like an animal. Mum, I'm sorry. I'm so sorry." He sobbed, unable to face the officer any longer. His mum gasped, then ran to his side to hold him, shushing him like a baby. It made him feel better, but only a little. He had opened the lid on a box he couldn't close.

PC Riaz sat silently for a moment, and Jude was glad when he turned his attention to Ashley. Ashley, by now, was furious, her fists pushing against each other in front of her mouth as she clearly tried to keep control of her temper. Jude had betrayed her. Instead of doing what they had agreed, he had done the opposite. Now he would have to wait and see what the consequences were.

"I don't know what the fuck he's on about," said Ashley. "He's lost the plot."

Jude's mum tutted. "Ashley! I don't know what's going on here, but we need to sort it out."

"I agree," said PC Riaz. "Lily Barnes? Are we talking about the same Lily Barnes who is well known to the police?"

"That girl is a menace." His mum shook her head. "The whole family is."

PC Riaz laced his fingers together on the table and sighed. "I've had a few run-ins with Lily Barnes, but did I hear you right, Jude? Did you say something happened to her? Did you say she was dead?"

Jude tried to stop sobbing. Snot ran down his lip and slipped into his mouth. He wiped himself with the back of his forearm and took a breath. "Y-Yes! We went back to the farmhouse to see the woman. She attacked Lily. She tore her throat out."

His mum covered her mouth. "Oh my God. What on earth have you kids got involved in? I think... I think I might need to call someone. You can't question them without a solicitor or something, right?"

PC Riaz put up a hand. "Nobody is under arrest here – yet – and this isn't an official interview. Let's just calm down and talk. This is all a little hard to stomach. If you kids say Lily Barnes is dead, then I need to know where she is, right now. Ashley, talk to me. I'm not your enemy, okay? If something's happened, then telling me is the best thing to do, I promise you."

Ashley shook her head. "I don't want to say anything."

PC Riaz turned his head. "Jude? Where is she? Where is Lily?"

"In the woods. She's at the farmhouse."

"And you say this woman attacked her? The same woman you saw yesterday? A woman of whom we found no evidence? Look, I really need you to take a moment to think about this before things go too far. There were no signs of anybody at that farmhouse. No chains, no blood. In fact, the only thing we found was your bracelet, Jude."

"I have her picture!" He fumbled with his pockets and pulled out his phone. A surge of excitement flooded through him as he realised he had evidence. He could prove he was telling the truth. "Here... look." He thumbed at his phone, opening the gallery and the images he had taken of Rose.

What? I don't understand.

The image he had taken of Rose showed only an empty room. Bare stone floors and crumbling brick walls. No symbols on the ground. No naked woman in chains.

Ashley was looking at him, a frown on her face. "Go on, Jude. Show them."

He tossed his phone on the table, revealing the useless picture. "I must have missed her. I don't..." His face lit up. "The locket! Ash, show them the locket."

Ashley looked at him and didn't say anything. To his surprise, she shrugged. "What locket?"

"The... The locket."

Ashley shrugged again.

Jude's mum squeezed his shoulder. "Tell the officer the truth, sweetheart. Stop whatever this is, right now, do you hear me? Ashley, what did you get Jude mixed up in?"

Ashley lurched back in her chair, a shocked expression on her face. "Did *I* get him mixed up in something? It was Jude's dumb idea to go back to the farmhouse. He wanted to be a hero and rescue the woman, but it turns out she's a goddamn psychopath. No wonder someone chained her up in the woods."

PC Riaz raised an eyebrow at her. "So you *did* see a woman? I thought you said you were mistaken."

"What? Yeah, well…" She stood up, knocking over her chair. "I'm done. You believe what you want, but I'm sick and tired of this."

"She wasn't mistaken," said Jude. "There was a woman in that farmhouse and her name is Rose. We went back to find her and she got free. Lily Barnes was with us, and Rose killed her. You need to go back to that farmhouse and arrest her before she hurts someone else. She's crazy. Right, Ashley?"

Ashley folded her arms and said nothing.

Jude sighed. "Please, officer. You need to believe us."

PC Riaz stood up. He went to speak but stopped himself, went to speak again but ended up shaking his head. After a moment's thought, he muttered to himself and left the kitchen. "I need to make a call. You kids better be worth the overtime."

Ashley glared at Jude, and he wondered if they would still be friends after this.

Ashley went home via police car for the second time in as many days. Fortunately, her dad was at work until 4 p.m., so PC Riaz had to speak with her mum. She had been too shocked to say anything besides, "Go to your room, young lady, and wait for your father to get home."

Ashley and Jude were on lockdown at each of the houses while the police investigated the woods, and two hours went by without Ashley knowing if the police had found anything. She spent the time in her bedroom, sitting cross-legged on her bed and staring at the wall. Thoughts ran through her mind like bees in her brain. Not only was her head full of horrifying images – Lily Barnes being torn apart and rotting children – but she was also furious at Jude. She tried not to hate him too much, but it was hard.

To distract herself, she opened the locket and examined the

children's smiling faces. The photographs were old, not quite black and white, but almost – like the sepia filter on her phone. She wished she had her phone now and wondered if her mum had taken it to the market yet. She wanted to talk to Jude, wanted to yell at him for being such a dumb fucking idiot. Now the police were investigating a murder, and she and Jude would most likely become the prime suspects. They hadn't found Rose the last time, and she had a grim feeling they wouldn't find her this time either. The woman possessed an impossible ability not to be seen. Lily Barnes didn't see her right until the moment her throat had been torn out. How was that possible? What was different about Lily that meant she hadn't been able to see Rose? How on earth was Lily like the police in that they could not see the woman either?

Ricky had seen her, though. In fact, he was the one other person who could back up their story. She hadn't mentioned his name to the police yet, not entirely sure why, but she wouldn't hesitate to get him involved if need be. No way was she going down for Lily's murder.

I'm glad she's dead.

If anybody deserved it, it was her.

As mad as she was at Jude for stabbing her in the back and not going along with the plan, she wanted to speak to him more than anyone else. He was her best friend and the only person who understood her – or at least the person who understood her most. She understood him too, which was why she knew he couldn't lie to a police officer. When PC Riaz glared at him and demanded answers, he had crumbled. Dishonesty just wasn't in Jude's nature, and she couldn't blame him for being who he was. Still, it would feel pretty good to give him a mouthful of abuse right about now.

Ashley stared at the clock for another half-hour, continuing to sit in silence. She waited for news, for PC Riaz to arrive and tell her she was right about everything and that they had caught Rose and placed her under arrest. But that didn't happen.

Instead, she flinched as the front door opened and her dad's voice sounded in the downstairs hallway. He already sounded grumpy, but his tone quickly worsened and his volume increased as he spoke to her mum in the kitchen. Then she heard his heavy footsteps on the stairs, loud and angry.

Ashley's bedroom door flew open and her dad stormed in, red-faced and seething. He pointed a finger at Ashley and growled. "What the hell have you got involved in, Ashley? Do you know how much trouble you're in? The police are looking for a dead girl because of you. You tell me everything you know, this instant."

Ashley's mum crept in behind her dad but kept silent.

Ashley hopped up off the bed, her heart pounding. "Dad, I swear, I didn't do anything. I only went back to look for the woman because the police couldn't find her. Jude and I wanted to prove she was there."

"Oh, so you two are kid detectives now, are you? The police said they found nothing, so why didn't you forget it? Why did you have to stir up trouble? What the hell happened to this Lily Barnes girl? You told the police she's been murdered."

Ashley shook her head desperately. "No, Jude said that. But it's true. The woman killed Lily. Rose killed her."

Her dad's eyes bulged. "You need help, Ashley. First thing tomorrow, you're going to see a doctor. You've been getting away with this kind of ridiculous behaviour for far too long. I don't work as hard as I do to—"

She groaned. "Oh, here we go again. Yeah, Dad, we all know how hard you work because you never stop telling us. Sorry that I was born, okay? Sorry that you have to feed me. Sorry you didn't get to open your stupid restaurant and live out your dreams. Sorry that—"

Ashley yelped as her dad slapped her across the face. She twisted and fell sideways onto her bed, bounced on the mattress and tumbled to the floor. He stood over her and glared, pointing a finger. "Don't you ever talk to me like that, young lady, do you hear me? I'll throw you out on the goddamn street."

Ashley's mother moved from the door and reached out a hand to him. "Honey, calm down. This isn't helping."

Ashley's dad threw an arm out and caught her mum across the chest. She cried out, more in fright than pain, and tumbled into the wall. "Quiet!" he yelled at her. "I'm sick to death of having to deal with everybody else's problems around here. Things are going to change. First of all, young lady, you are never to see Jude again. His mother is an alcoholic, and he's clearly bad news too. It's time you got some proper friends. Other girls."

Ashley felt something warm on her face and realised it was blood trickling from her nose. She was terrified, but she was angry too.

So fucking angry.

She leapt to her feet and got in her dad's face, which was a foot and a half higher than hers. "I will not stop seeing Jude. He's my best friend, and the only person who gives two shits about me."

"You'll do as you're told while you live under my roof."

"Fuck you!"

Her dad raised his palm to hit her again.

Ashley flinched and brought up her hands to defend herself. But the slap never came.

Gingerly, she lowered her arms. Her dad had turned away and was holding his face. He was bleeding. Immediately, Ashley's mum rushed over to him and started making a fuss. "Honey, your nose is bleeding."

Ashley wiped away the blood coming from her nose and wondered how her dad was suddenly bleeding as well. She hadn't fought him, so what had happened?

Even though distracted, he was still angry. He shoved Ashley's mum away and grunted. Blood dripped from the end of his nose. "Probably my blood pressure," he said, trying to stem the flow with the back of his hand. "All the stress you two cause me."

Ashley's mum continued to fuss over her dad, despite the aggression he showed towards her. "It's really gushing," she fretted. "Come on, honey, let's get you to the bathroom."

Ashley stood in silence while her parents exited her bedroom. She asked herself why the hell her mum was fussing over her dad when she had a nosebleed too. And hers wasn't accidental.

Her dad had never hit her before, and she didn't quite know what to do. Lately, it was as though he was a stranger – or at least slowly turning into one. It made her afraid to be in her own home.

I hate him.

I fucking hate him.

She couldn't stay in this house. She couldn't cope with everything in addition to her dad hitting her.

I'm out of here.

Ashley hurried downstairs and headed out the front door.

CHAPTER FIFTEEN

"I CAN'T BELIEVE we haven't heard anything," said Jude.

It'd been over four hours since PC Riaz had left to take Ashley home. Before leaving, the officer had ordered Jude to remain with his mum. For once, she was being strict with him and had forbidden him from using his phone or going up to his room where she couldn't see him.

Currently, Jude was sitting in the kitchen opposite his mum. The cordless landline phone lay on the table between them and they both stared at it. PC Riaz had promised to call as soon as he knew anything. Despite his reluctance to believe their story, he had at least taken it seriously.

Jude wondered if Lily's family had been contacted yet. He really didn't want a run-in with that bunch of lunatics. Part of him held a sliver of hope that the police might find Lily alive, but he knew, deep down, it was impossible. No way could she have survived after losing so much blood.

"I'm sure we'll get an update soon." His mum reached out and patted his hand. She looked at him with bleary eyes. In the last couple of hours, she'd drunk an entire bottle of white wine. She kept shaking her head and muttering under her breath. Every now and then she would look up and smile. "Everything will be okay. I... I just don't understand what on earth you and Ashley have got yourselves mixed up in."

Jude slumped onto the table and buried his face in his hands. "I don't want to go over it all again, Mum. We did nothing wrong. The only reason we were even in the woods was because Ricky Dalca and Lily Barnes chased us in there. If I could take it all back, I would, Mum, but the woman we saw – Rose, she's..." He couldn't get the words out. He tried to swallow a lump in his throat.

His mum blinked at him, sniffed, then blinked again. "She's what, sweetheart?"

"Evil, Mum. I think she's evil. Like, an *actual* monster."

She patted his hand again. "Try not to get carried away. You're safe, and I believe you."

"No, you don't! I overheard you on the phone last night. You think I'm mental."

She frowned and acted as though she didn't understand what he was talking about. Perhaps she didn't. She'd been drunk last night, too.

"Mum? Answer me!"

She reached out and took his hand in hers. Her pupils were large. "Jude, listen to me. I admit, I'm not really sure what to think right now, but I know my son. I might not be a perfect mum, but you're a perfect son – and you've never been a liar. Never have you hurt anybody. Whatever's going on, I know it can't have been your fault. Is that enough?"

A maelstrom rose in the space behind his nose and eyes. It resulted in an explosion of tears. His mum scooted around the table on her chair and pulled him into a hug. Then he let go completely, and all the emotions from the last forty-eight hours erupted from his lungs. Ricky's punches. Lily's taunts. The chained woman he thought had been a victim but had revealed herself to be a monster. Now the police were searching the woods, and things would probably only get worse. Right now, he just wanted to hide in his mum's arms. He wanted to be a cuddled child.

A loud knock at the door startled them.

Jude pulled back away from his mum and realised she had been crying too. She wiped at her tears, embarrassed, then stood from the table. With a huff, she straightened herself up. "That must be the police. They'll be buying us a new front door if they keep banging on it like that."

Jude reached out to her. "Mum..."

She turned and wiped his tears away with her thumbs, then kissed his forehead. "It'll be okay, sweetheart. I'm here."

Jude sat trembling at the breakfast table while his mum answered the door. He pictured PC Riaz marching in to arrest him, charging him with the murder of Lily Barnes.

What if Ashley told them it was me to save herself? She already screwed me over by lying about the locket. She was angry with me.

But she would never do that to me. She wouldn't let me take the blame.

This is all because of Rose. Please let the police find her.

Butterflies took flight in Jude's stomach as his mum opened the door. He listened to her greet the person who had knocked. "Oh, it's you!" she said. "Come on in. Have you heard anything?"

Jude relaxed when Ashley stepped into the hallway. His mum closed the front door and ushered her into the kitchen, where she sat at the table and nodded a 'hello' to Jude. Her nose appeared swollen, and there was a small cut on the bridge. Her lips were red like she'd been sucking on an ice lolly. It was blood. "Whoa!" he said. "What happened?"

She was holding back tears, and her tone was angry when she answered the question. "My dad hit me. Smacked me right in the face while my mum stood there and watched. He hit her, too, but she just accepted it. I can't be in that house anymore. I... I can't."

Jude's mum had a hand over her mouth and gasped. "Jesus, Ashley, I'm so sorry. Let me get you cleaned up." She hurried over to the oven and yanked the purple tea towel hanging from its long silver handle. After running it under the warm tap, she brought it over to Ashley.

Jude sat silently while his mum saw to his friend.

Once the blood was all cleaned up, Ashley relaxed. "Thanks, Helen. I'm sorry to come here. I just... I didn't know where else to go."

Jude's mum put a hand on her back and rubbed. "Tempers are high at the moment, but you're part of the family, Ashley. If you need a safe place to go, you're always welcome here."

A single tear escaped Ashley's eye and tumbled down her cheek. She swatted it like a fly and snorted. "I don't even know what's real right now. I feel like this is a dream I can't wake up from."

Jude nodded. He was constantly having to sniff to keep back snot, and his eyes were itching with spent tears, but he managed half a smile. "Tell me about it. I keep thinking back to a few days ago when everything was normal. We were bored, remember?"

Ashley chuckled. "Yeah, give me bored any day." Then she grew serious, her teary eyes hardening. "I wish we'd never gone into those woods, Jude. Damn Ricky and Lily for chasing us in there. This is all their fault. Ricky and Lily are to blame; they always are. Shit... what am I saying? Lily's dead, and I'm angry at her. You'd think I'd let it go."

Jude had no idea what to say. He watched his mum pull another bottle of wine from the fridge and unscrew the cap. She kept her back to him as she poured a fresh glass. One bottle was usually her limit.

"Mum, I know you said I couldn't go to my room, but—"

She waved an arm back at him. "Yes, okay, I suppose we could all do with a break. If I hear anything, I'll shout you."

"Thanks."

Jude was glad to get out of the kitchen, so he grabbed

Ashley's arm and pulled her up out of her chair. The two of them headed through the hall and up the stairs. When Jude opened the door to his room, he immediately felt calmer. This was his place. He was safe here.

Although I wasn't safe last night, was I? I wasn't safe when my bath turned to ice and my television showed me those children getting stabbed.

Somehow Rose got to me. Ashley, too. We're not safe in our homes.

Is Rose going to come for us tonight?

Jude moved over to his desk and picked up a magic wand that he used as part of his magic shows. There was a secret cap on one end for pulling out handkerchiefs or small red balls. "I wish this was real," he said, only half joking. "We could stick Rose back inside her triangle."

Ashley nodded. "Yeah, I could use a little magic about now."

Jude tossed the wand back onto the desk, knowing childish fantasies wouldn't help him. They needed to approach this rationally, if that was even possible. There had to be something that could help them.

Ashley took a seat on the bed, but Jude remained standing as it occurred to him that they had something that didn't belong to them. "Ash, do you still have Rose's pendant?"

She frowned at him. "You mean the locket? Yeah, I have it in my pocket, I think."

"Show it to me."

Ashley leant sideways on the bed and slid a hand into her pocket. She pulled the locket out and held it in her palm. Instinctively, Jude reached out to take it, but he recoiled. The fact it belonged to Rose was enough to dissuade him from wanting anything to do with it. It was probably cursed.

A witch's trinket.

This isn't a game. There's no such thing as real magic. Is there?

I took Rose's picture. I'm sure of it.

The locket was exactly as he remembered it: a delicate chain with a thick chunk of metal at its centre. Gold in colour, but not actually gold. It was something else.

Ashley opened the locket and revealed the photographs inside. Jude was certain the two children were the same ones he'd seen on television. The mother, who had stabbed them to death, however, hadn't looked like Rose.

"Rose isn't the woman who I saw kill the children," he said. "It was a woman with dark hair."

Ashley sighed, and a whistle escaped her swollen nose. "Rose has dark hair. I mean, she has blonde hair, but there was this moment back at the farmhouse, when the flash on your phone went off, that she changed. The whole room changed, and when I looked at her, her hair was darker. She looked like a totally different person. I think she changed her appearance to trick us. She wanted to look like a desperate woman, but that's the last thing she is."

Jude frowned. "My phone didn't capture anything when I took a picture. How is that possible?"

"Rose can stop herself from being seen. Lily didn't see her until it was too late, and the police didn't see her either. I think she's... you know...?"

Jude shook his head. "What?"

"Well..." She chewed her lip for a moment between words. "She's not a normal person, is she? She's, like, a witch or something. Maybe a vampire with the way she was biting Lily. She was eating her."

Hearing the words out loud was both a relief and a terrifying reality check. Jude had hoped the madness was only inside his head, but it clearly wasn't. Ashley was trapped in this nightmare too.

He deflated and sat on the bed beside her. Their upper arms pressed against each other, and he enjoyed the feeling of her warm body against his. Whatever happened, they were in it together. They were on the same side.

"I'm sorry I didn't stick with the plan," he said. "I know we agreed to stay quiet, but when PC Riaz started questioning me, I just..."

Ashley put a hand on his thigh, which sent a tingle from his knee to his groin. "An hour ago, I wanted to chew you up and spit you out," she said, "but the truth is you were just being you, and that's okay. I can't blame you for wanting to be honest – it's in your nature – so... we're cool."

Jude managed a smile. "One down, two down."

"One down, two down."

They sat for a few seconds in silence until Jude spoke again. "I'm worried Rose is going to come back for her locket. She told Ricky it belonged to her. It sounded like a threat."

Ashley thumbed the locket closed and ran a finger over its dull metal surface. "I'm worried about that too. She was completely naked but still wearing this. Doesn't that strike you as odd? Huh, I suppose everything about this is odd, right? I just want to hear from PC Riaz and know what happens next."

"We should have told him about Ricky. I almost did, but then I had flashbacks about him kicking my ass. Maybe after covering for him, he'll finally leave me alone."

"If he doesn't, at least you'll have something to threaten him with." She turned and looked at the alarm clock on his night-stand. It was shaped like a crystal ball, with the readout floating in the middle. "Why haven't we had an update yet? There must be people searching the farmhouse by now. I wonder who it even belongs to."

Jude nodded thoughtfully. Surely the run-down ruin of a farmhouse didn't have an owner. It must have belonged to the council or been forgotten about completely. The old building certainly was a mystery, but as much as he enjoyed the idea of an adventure, he decided the real thing wasn't much fun. He would stick to books and films and playing video games on his laptop.

My laptop.

"Hey, why don't we look it up? Maybe we can find something on the Net."

Ashley grimaced. "Not sure I even want to know."

But Jude was excited. Excited by the possibility of knowing more than they did right now. The most terrifying thing about their ordeal was the complete lack of understanding, but perhaps there was a way to make sense of things.

He reached under his bed and pulled out his chunky old laptop. Placing it on the bed, he opened it up and powered it on. The ancient computer took a good five minutes to wake up. Once it had, it was good to go. He brought up the web browser and search bar.

"What should I type?"

Ashley shrugged. "No idea. Old farmhouses and our town?"

It wasn't much to go on, but Jude did his best to narrow things down. Eventually, he started searching for anything about farms around where the golf course was. Most of the results were articles about the golf course itself or adverts for restaurants. Then, right near the bottom of the page, there was a snippet that made Jude take notice.

Redsow pig farm to make way for town's first golf course.

The reason the article was so far down was because it had been written in 1968. When he clicked the link, it wasn't even an article but a scanned image of the local newspaper's front page on that date.

Jude nudged Ashley, although she was staring right at the screen alongside him. "This is it!" he said. "Look at the picture."

Ashley squinted at the screen and studied the image for a moment. There was only a single image on the newspaper's front page and it was poor quality – the overzealous blacks obliterating the muddy greys and whites. It was clear, however, that they were looking at an image of an old farmhouse. The curious thing was that it was already dilapidated. The roof was still on, but several parts of the brick wall were missing.

Ashley pointed a finger at the screen. "It says here that the pig farm closed down in 1948. Wow, it really is old."

"So it was abandoned for twenty years, and they just built the golf course around it. They left it there and allowed the woods to grow around it."

"And it lay forgotten until we went and disturbed it." She shook her head. "We're so dumb."

"Someone else was there before us, Ash. Whoever chained Rose up inside."

Ashley arched her back and stretched, her large breasts flattening and spreading out. "Does it say anything about who owns it?"

"Let me check." He tutted. "Only the front page has been scanned. The rest of the article isn't here. Wait, hold on... It says the pig farm was operated by the Glendale family. The sale of the land was approved by... a Rita Glendale."

"Great," said Ashley, but she pulled a face. "This was all in 1968, though, right? So this Rita will be dead by now."

Jude didn't answer her. He was on a trail, which was something he enjoyed. Many times in the past he had become interested in a subject and followed the breadcrumbs across the Internet in search of answers. He entered 'Rita Glendale' into the search bar and hit enter.

Something came up immediately.

He clicked the first article.

"Says here she was the town's first female councillor. Wow, she was in charge of our ward."

Ashley frowned. "What does that mean? She was like a politician or something?"

"Yeah, she used to help run this part of town, like a representative or something. There's a picture of her here from the eighties. Look."

The two of them studied the faded picture of a bony woman with curly grey hair. In the photograph, she was holding a young boy against her side. The caption explained it was her son, Peter, an avid young artist. A chalk picture of some daffodils had been drawn on the pavement. It was pretty good if the kid had drawn it.

"She had a son. Peter Glendale."

Ashley scratched at the inside of her nostril, grossly dislodging some dried blood. "So maybe we search for this Peter, then? Although, if his mum sold the farm before he was even born, he probably doesn't know any more than we do."

Once again, Jude followed the breadcrumbs. He typed in 'Peter Glendale' and tapped enter.

There were no articles about Peter, but he was listed as a company director on a government website. It looked like he owned some kind of marketing agency, but the crazy thing was, the website listed his home address.

Jude gasped. "He lives here. Packer Street. Isn't that down near the supermarket?"

Ashley nodded. "Yeah, my mum used to clean for a lady down there. Nice houses."

"Do you reckon he could help us? Do you think he has any idea who Rose is?"

Ashley shook her head. "No. It happened too long ago. Why would he?"

Jude was about to conduct another Internet search, but a loud banging at the front door interrupted him. His mum yelled up the stairs for him to come down.

He looked at Ashley. "The police, you think?"

"Dunno."

They went over to the bedroom door and stepped out onto the landing. Rather than head downstairs, they eavesdropped.

It was Ashley's father. "Is she here?" he said, sounding tired. "I just need to talk with her, Helen."

"I think you've done enough talking for tonight, Tony. She wants to be left alone. She's perfectly safe here, for now, so leave her be."

"She needs to come home with me. She needs to be home when the police come back. This has all gone way too far."

"I agree, but she said you hit her."

"That's... It's not like it sounds."

"Jesus, Tony."

"Keep your nose out of my business. Go pour yourself another drink and leave my daughter to me."

"How dare you!"

"You're pissed. My daughter isn't staying here."

There was the brief sound of a scuffle followed by Jude's mum grunting. When she spoke again, she was angry. "Come inside my house and I'll have you locked up, Tony, do you understand? You might knock your own family about, but you're not gunna play that game with me. Ashley's here because she's upset, so just give the poor girl some space. I'll take care of her tonight and call you in the morning. If the police arrive, I'll talk to them, okay?"

"No, not okay. I want my daughter."

"You're not coming in."

There was the sound of another scuffle and Ashley raced halfway down the stairs. When Ashley's dad saw her, his face lit up. "Ashley? I need you to come home. We need to talk about things."

"No, we don't. Leave me alone, Dad."

He sighed and leant against the door frame. His right foot was inside the hallway. "I'm sorry for losing my temper, okay, but you need to come home. You need to face the mess you've made."

Ashley hissed. "Are you for real? The mess I've made? All

Jude and I have done is the right thing. It's everybody else who's fucked up. I'm not coming home, Dad. Just go."

Her dad pushed himself away from the door frame and barged into Jude's mum. She yelped in surprise and fell against the wall but threw out a hip to keep him from getting past. The two of them started wrestling.

Ashley screamed and ran down the rest of the stairs. She paused in the hallway to point a finger at her grunting, red-faced dad. "Just fucking leave me alone!"

Jude didn't know what to do. His mum was fighting with everything she had to keep Ashley's dad out. Meanwhile, Ashley fled into the kitchen. "Mum, I-I'm going to call the police, okay? Hold on."

"Yes! Call 999," she begged. "Tell them I'm being attacked."

Ashley's dad gave up the struggle and moved back outside. He adjusted his misshapen shirt and growled. "Fine. I'm going, okay? But you tell Ashley I want her home. Tonight. Or I'll be the one calling the police."

"Get the hell out of here, Tony."

Jude raced into the kitchen, intending to tell Ashley that her dad was leaving, but when he got there, he found the kitchen empty and the back door wide open. Ashley had gone.

The sun was shining outside, and Jude had to blink to adjust his vision. Ashley couldn't have gone far because she had entered the kitchen only ten seconds before he had, and sure enough, he found her marching through the alleyway at the end of his close. The alleyway led to the playground, which was where he figured she was heading. The small park was away from the roads, which meant her dad wouldn't catch up to her in his car.

Jude felt bad for leaving his mum, but his priority right now was Ashley. She was afraid of her own dad, which he couldn't possibly imagine, having barely ever known his own. Even so, he couldn't imagine being afraid of a parent. His mum had plenty of issues, but he never doubted that she loved him.

Jude caught up to Ashley as she exited the alleyway. She'd seen him coming, having peeked over her shoulder at the sound of his hurried footsteps, but she didn't say anything as he joined her. She stared ahead in silence.

This used to be so much easier. We always used to know the right thing to say to one another.

"I love you, Ash. You're my best friend, and I'm sorry you're having to deal with all this shit on top of everything else. I didn't realise things had got so bad with your dad."

"Not your fault. Just the way it is."

And that was the end of the conversation. They walked until they reached the playground, and when they saw somebody sitting there alone, they grimaced.

Ricky was slumped with his head between his knees and a mostly empty bottle of cider at his side. Jude was disinclined to disturb him, but Ashley decided differently and called out, "Hey, Ricky? What are you doing here on your own?"

He flinched and looked at them. His brown hair was a mess and his eyelids were sagging. He said nothing until Jude and Ashley were inside the playground's railings. "Did you tell the police anything about me?" he slurred.

"We didn't tell 'em anything," said Ashley, "Have you heard anything? Have the police found Lily?"

Ricky pulled a face and let out a silent belch. He reeked of alcohol, and it wafted towards them on his breath. "The plods were all over the fucking place earlier," he said. "They went into the woods, and to Lily's house too. Her family's on the warpath. If they find out we left Lily to die out there in the woods, we're fucked. We're all fucking fucked."

Jude leant against the railings and folded his arms. It wasn't cold, but he felt a shiver. "We weren't the ones who hurt Lily. It was Rose. You need to tell the police you saw her, too. They need to catch her."

Ricky said nothing. He picked up his bottle of cider and took a swig.

Ashley moved directly in front of him. For a moment, she stared at the top of his head. Then she rolled her eyes. "You're a complete mess, Ricky. If the police question you, how are you going to keep your story straight? We might need you to back us up. If the police don't find Rose, they're going to start looking for other answers."

Ricky tried to look up at her, but he couldn't keep his head still and his eyes were all over the place. "You don't say nothing about me to the police, you get me? I'll fucking kill you if you drag me into this."

"You dragged yourself into this," said Jude, "when you marched me back to the farmhouse. If you'd just let me call for help, you wouldn't have got involved in anything. In fact, if anybody is to blame for what happened to Lily, it's you."

Ricky stood up and took an unsteady step towards Jude at the railing. "The fuck you say to me?"

Ashley grabbed Ricky's arm and pulled him away from Jude. "You weren't to blame, Ricky. It isn't fair for Jude to say that, but we're done with you and your threats, okay? You ever lay a finger on Jude again, I'll kill you."

Ricky glared at her and took a step so that he was right inside her personal space. He leant forward so that his face was up against hers. "I'd like to see you try, flabby tits. Maybe we could even have some fun. You should ditch this prick and hang with me. I'll show you what a real man's like."

Ashley rolled her eyes and spat on the floor. "You spend so much time telling other people they're losers, Ricky, but the funny thing is, you're the biggest loser of all. You're a train wreck waiting to happen, and if you were the last person on Earth, I still wouldn't hang out with you. If you can't be a normal human being, then just leave us both the fuck alone."

"And what if I don't? What if I kick the shit out of Judy right here and now? What if I put him in hospital with a feeding tube? You going to do something about it?"

"Don't test me."

Ricky chuckled, then turned clumsily and took a step towards Jude. Ashley's tough bitch act had been impressive, but Ricky was clearly incapable of good behaviour.

He's going to hit me. It's happened enough times for me to know. What do I do? I really can't cope with it anymore.

Ricky got right in Jude's face. It was the usual tactic of glaring at him and making him squirm, but this time Jude didn't squirm. He put both hands on Ricky's chest and pushed him away firmly. In his drunken state, Ricky staggered and almost fell, but it only made him angrier. He clenched both hands into fists and glared at Jude. "Oh, you're a dead man now. I'm going to stamp on your fucking balls till there's nothing left. That's if you even have any."

"Leave him alone." Ashley grabbed Ricky's arm again and spun him.

Ricky lashed out. He shoved Ashley away and raised his fist. The sight of him threatening her caused Jude to yell out in anger. He shoved himself away from the railings and threw himself towards Ricky.

Ashley threw up her arms to defend herself.

Ricky recoiled, then squealed like a stuck pig. He doubled over in pain and screamed. "My hand! My fucking hand."

Jude had still been a metre away, his attempt to stop Ricky from punching Ashley likely to fail, but something had happened that prevented the assault. Ricky was in agony. He kept on screaming about his hand.

Ashley was visibly confused. "What is it? What's happened?"

Ricky stopped screaming and bit down on his lip. He looked at Ashley and threw out his hand for her to see. It had shrivelled up like the clumps of ginger his mum kept in the cupboard beside the fridge. His fingers were twisted, his palm withered like the skin of a rotting peach. Even as they stared at it, Ricky's hand curled in on itself even more.

Ashley and Jude exchanged a glance. Ricky had been about

to punch her, but instead his hand had been destroyed. It didn't seem a coincidence. Jude looked at Ashley and tried to figure out what the hell had happened. "He was going to hurt you. What stopped him?"

Ashley's face had grown pale, and she stared at him. Slowly, she reached a hand into her jeans pocket and pulled out Rose's locket. She tried to speak but faltered and had to start again. "M-My dad gave me a nosebleed. Then his nose started bleeding."

Jude understood immediately what she was saying. "Because of the locket. It's... It's more than just a piece of jewellery, isn't it?"

Ashley stared at the piece of old jewellery hanging from her trembling hand. "I think so."

Ricky went back to screaming, and took off in a panic, which was hardly surprising. Jude couldn't imagine how afraid he must be. He was a victim of witchcraft or some kind of evil spell. Would his hand stay that way forever?

Maybe Rose isn't evil. So far, the only people she's hurt are Ricky and Lily. Bullies.

Ashley and Jude stood in the playground, stunned. There was seemingly no end to the nightmare in which they found themselves. How much more misery would go around before it was over?

"We need help," said Jude, "before more people get hurt."

Ashley nodded. She still held the locket but wouldn't dare look at it.

Jude leant against the railing, needing to take a breather. "If this were a movie, what would be our next move?"

"This isn't a movie, Jude, so stop being an idiot."

"I'm not being stupid. We don't have any other frame of reference, so why not a movie? What would our next move be?"

She put a hand against her forehead and groaned. "Jesus, I don't know. We don't even understand what's going on. I suppose we would go off in search of answers, visit the local library and go through old newspapers, or look for clues at a museum. Shit, maybe we would go ask Dora the fucking Explorer. Like I said, this isn't a movie."

Jude huffed. He knew he was being stupid, but sometimes he found it easier to think in plotlines. He enjoyed order, and movies and books always followed a formula. Perhaps life did too; he would certainly like to think so. Then it came to him. He smiled at Ashley, which only seemed to annoy her.

"Why are you grinning? Ricky lost his freaking hand because of me."

"You were right. If this were a movie, we would go looking for answers. What's the one lead we have? The one piece of information we have that might lead to more information?"

Ashley shrugged. She clearly didn't want to play along.

"Peter Glendale. We have his address. His family is connected to the farmhouse. Maybe he'll know who Rose is."

"We've already been through this. There's no way he could know anything. The farmhouse hasn't belonged to his family in fifty years. Longer."

"Well, what else do we have? If we stick around here doing nothing, more bad things are going to happen. Either the police will come and arrest us, or your dad will find us. Maybe Lily's family. And what happens to the next person who gets nasty with you? Ricky's hand might only be the start."

Ashley held up the locket. "I'll get rid of this. Then there's no problem."

"It's more than that and you know it. Rose came for us last night before you even got hold of that locket. She's been after us since the moment we first met her. This doesn't end until we understand who she is and what she wants. We need to go see Peter Glendale, because that's the only thing we can do."

Ashley folded her arms and looked unhappy. It was her usual expression, and it was comforting to see it return. She shrugged. "Okay, so we walk to his house and hope he's there. It'll take us, what, two hours? Then what if he doesn't want to talk to us? Or if he decides we're crazy and calls the police?"

"Then we're in no worse position than we are now. What do we have to lose?"

Ashley moved towards the playground's exit. "Okay, then I guess we start walking."

And so they did. Neither knew a way to get to Peter Glendale's house via the footpaths, so they followed the main road, walking along the verge and stomping through the unmowed summer grass. Several times, Ash thought she saw her dad's car coming and ducked into the weeds, but every time it turned out to be a false alarm. Eventually, she started to relax.

It was nice to just walk for a while, to get away from the playground and the woods and their parents. Jude even pretended in his mind that they were outlaws, fleeing the police and the murder and mayhem left in their wake. The problem was, things rarely turned out well for outlaws.

Walking on the grassy embankments alongside the main roads was tiring, and after an hour, Jude's shins ached. Ashley was shorter than he was, and she had sweated a little through the back of her T-shirt. He imagined her moist skin, and a picture of her, naked and panting, appeared unbidden in his mind. It was bizarre and unwanted, and not how he had ever thought about her. They had always been close, but after the last few days, they had become more than friends. They were allies now. Allies against a world that seemed to have it in for them.

After another ten minutes of walking, they came to a wider embankment covered in daffodils. The cluster of yellow splashes caused them to stop and admire the flowers. Ashley knelt and picked one, bringing it to her swollen nose and inhaling deeply. She didn't say what she was thinking, but it brought a smile to her face. Behind that smile, however, was nothing but sadness.

Jude stood next to her. "It's going to be okay, you know. I mean, there has to be an end to this. None of this is our fault."

She surprised him by leaning forward and wrapping both arms around him. She hugged him tightly and rested her head on his shoulder. "I wish I could believe you, but everything about this tells me it's all gunna go very badly for us. Our whole lives, it's been you and me, Jude, but it's not normal. We can't just be two kids in our own little world anymore. We have to join the real world – and the real world sucks. In the real world, our friendship doesn't get to be everything. There has to be more."

Jude held onto her hug, not wanting to break away. It felt good to hold her, but something seemed fragile about it, like there was something between them that could fall to the ground and smash at any moment. "What do you mean? We'll always be friends, right?"

Ashley broke away and looked at him. She nodded, but there were tears in her eyes. "Of course. Come on, we're almost there."

They carried on walking but didn't say another word until they reached the supermarket that marked their destination. Across the main road was a posh housing district. The street they were looking for was only a ten-minute walk. Soon, they would arrive at the house of Peter Glendale.

CHAPTER SIXTEEN

WHEN THEY FINALLY REACHED PACKER STREET, IT was evening. The day was trying to cling on stubbornly, but it was fighting a losing battle. Only a slither of orange sunlight remained and it was quickly sinking behind the horizon.

Only nine or ten houses lined the upmarket cul-de-sac, and each one was huge. All had double garages, and several had gated driveways. Jude was unnerved when he realised the biggest house of all was the one they wanted.

Ashley whistled. "Peter's got money. Wonder if he's single."

"Might be a bit old for you, Ash."

"I could do with a sugar daddy. Might save me from having to go home again."

Jude gave her a thin-lipped smile. "You'll sort things out with your dad, Ash, I'm sure. "

"The fucker hit me. How do you sort that out?"

"I... I don't know. Maybe you can come live at mine."

She rolled her eyes. "What? In your mum's room or yours?"

Jude blushed. "Yeah, I suppose we don't really have the room, do we?"

"No, but thanks. I know you're just trying to help me.

Anyway, I don't want to even think about it right now. We're here, so let's do what we came to do."

They stood in front of the wooden gate that barred the short driveway in front of a large Tudor-style house that looked big enough to encompass Jude's house six times over.

"There's a buzzer here," said Ashley, pointing to a small grey panel on one side of the gate.

Jude shivered against the cold. Now that they were here, it seemed like a really stupid idea. They were about to press a rich person's buzzer and ask about a witch named Rose who lived in the woods on the other side of town. Even if they didn't mention Rose, they still planned to ask about a ruined old farmhouse that had been forgotten fifty-odd years ago. Suddenly, he couldn't see a scenario where this went well.

Ashley pressed the buzzer.

A male voice answered almost right away. "Hello?"

"Um, is that Peter Glendale?"

"Yes, can I help you?"

Jude looked at Ashley and realised they hadn't discussed what they planned to say. "Um, we..."

Ashley took the reins. "Hi, Mr Glendale. We're doing a school project and the topic is local history. Do you know anything about an old farmhouse near the golf course? We read an old news article that mentioned it belonging to a Rita Glendale. Is she related to you?"

There was a pause, and for a moment it seemed like there might not be an answer. Then the male speaker replied, "That's my grandmother, but I'm not sure about the farmhouse you're talking about. Rita grew up on a farm, but it was before I was born."

"That's right," said Jude, gaining confidence from Ashley's good start. "The farm was sold in 1968 to make way for the golf course. Any information you might have on it would really help us. It's going to count towards our final GCSE grade."

"Who were you again?"

"My name is Jude, and my friend is Ashley. It's just a school project."

Another long pause, this one stretching out for half a minute. Then: "You'd better come in."

Jude couldn't help but smile. Once again, he felt like an adventurer, and this time they were making progress.

The gate's hinges clicked, and the whole thing opened. Jude put his hand on the top plank and gave it a push. It swung aside easily. Then they were walking up the driveway and heading towards the large home of a complete stranger.

The driveway was lined on either side by flowerbeds, each one full of colourful summer flowers. Beside the dark timber-framed front door was a tiny wheelbarrow full of even more flowers. It was a beautiful home and had a nice friendly feel to it. It made Jude slightly less apprehensive that Peter Glendale would do anything besides help them.

He has to have answers. He's our only hope.

The man who opened the front door appeared to be in his early forties, not much younger than Jude's mum. His short brown hair had a strict parting on the left. He looked at them from behind stylish black glasses, and while he seemed a little confused by the sight of them, he smiled warmly.

"I'm Ashley. This is Jude. Thank you for talking to us."

"Sure, no problem. I'm not really sure how I can help you, but please come in." He moved aside and allowed them in. The hallway's wooden floors were a rich honey colour. The walls were a pale shade of green. "You have a beautiful home, Mr Glendale."

"Thank you. It actually belonged to my parents, but they both passed away in recent years. It's the family home, though, so I wasn't ready to sell it. I should've filled it with children by now, really, but that's a story for another day. Can I get you kids a drink? Water, Coke? Or would you prefer tea?"

Jude grew anxious as the front door closed and locked behind him, so he asked for a cup of tea, knowing it would calm him. Ashley went with a glass of water. She must have been as thirsty as he was after the two-hour walk.

Peter led them through into the kitchen, which was even nicer than the hallway. The cream cabinets were topped by a thick wooden worktop that matched the hallway floor. The tiles underfoot were a mixture of browns and oranges. Like the rest of the house so far, it had a warm and inviting feel.

Definitely a family home.

But what kind of family?

There was no breakfast table in the kitchen, but a pair of stools stood against one side of the counter. Peter motioned for them both to take a seat, and Jude hopped up onto one of the stools. He accepted a cup of tea gratefully and wrapped his hands around the ceramic mug, enjoying the warmth. Ashley sat beside him, sipping her water. For a few moments, nobody said anything. Eventually, Peter spoke. "So tell me about this farmhouse? You say my grandmother used to own it?"

Ashley put her water on a nearby drinks mat and nodded. "We read a newspaper article on the Internet that said she sold it in 1968 so they could build the golf course. Although it also said that the farmhouse had been empty since 1948. Do you know why it was abandoned?"

Peter shook his head. "No idea. My grandmother grew up on a farm, but she never really spoke about it. It was her parent's place, I think, and they retired shortly after the war. I don't think she ever really enjoyed the work. She got involved in town planning instead. Did you know she helped develop most of this town? Until the nineteen-eighties, it was actually only a collection of tiny villages. Eventually, they all merged into the town we know today."

Jude nodded appreciatively. It genuinely interested him how much places could change over time. He imagined the space where his house was, a hundred years ago. It was probably just a field back then. "That must have been an amazing job," he said. "Did you know your grandmother well?"

Peter's face lit up with a beaming smile. "Oh, yes. We were very close. I was probably closer to my grandmother than I was my own mother. My mother was a doctor, you see, so she spent a lot of hours at the hospital, but my grandmother was always around when I was a kid. In fact, it was she who taught me how to draw, which is how I make my living today. I run a marketing and ad agency from home, using the very skills she taught me. So, yes, my grandmother and I are very close."

Jude frowned. "Sorry, did you just say *are* very close?"

Peter gave them a cheeky grin. Even though he was middle-aged, there was something childish about him. He had an air of mischief. "Okay, you got me. I had to check you kids out first, but my grandmother is still very much alive if you'd like to speak to her."

Ashley gasped. "She's still alive? How old is she?"

"She's ninety-six, but still as sharp as a tack. When she heard you on the intercom, she told me to let you in. She's willing to talk to you."

Jude and Ashley gawked at one another. After two days of everything going wrong, things were finally going right. They had come to speak with Peter Glendale about his grandmother, but instead they would get a chance to talk to the woman herself. Rita Glendale had owned the farmhouse. If anybody knew anything about the old place, it was her. Jude crossed his fingers and prayed she also knew something about Rose.

Peter gestured to a door at the rear of the kitchen. "Grab your drinks and come this way. She's a little hard of hearing, so you'll have to speak up. And watch your language. She'll tan your hides if she hears you swearing."

Their host led them from the kitchen into a small sitting room lit by several floor lamps. Inside, slumped in a dark brown leather recliner, was an old lady. Her hair was pure white and her face a tapestry of wrinkles, but she was the same woman they had seen in the photograph in the paper on the Internet. Across her lap was a patchwork of coloured wool. When she saw them enter, she placed a pair of knitting needles onto a small side table and smiled. Various trinkets lined the walls, all of them odd. Jude noticed a pair of tiny wooden hammers and a metal ring covered in a sinewy reed. There was also a strange twisted tree branch pinned against the longest wall between a pair of white eyeless masks. Strange decorations, for sure, yet they all tied together to create a pleasant enough sitting room.

The old woman lifted a pair of spectacles from where they hung around her neck and placed them on her nose. She examined Jude and Ashley carefully, like she was inspecting them for work duty. Then, once she was satisfied, she gave them a curt nod and told them to sit on the small fabric sofa opposite. Jude felt like a naughty child waiting to speak with the headmaster.

"What do you lambies know about my family's old farmhouse?" the old woman asked them in a voice that sounded like duelling whispers. "That place has been buried in the woods for half a century or more."

"Or more," said Jude. "You sold it in 1968."

The old woman seemed to think about it before nodding. "I suppose I did. Glad to see the back of the old place, to tell the truth. It was a ruin long before I passed it on. The farming life never suited me."

Standing near the door, Peter chuckled.

"You sold it to the council," said Jude. "Why didn't they knock it down when they built the golf course?"

"Never sold it to the council, lamby. Sold it to a real estate company. I remember it well because they had the stupidest name you ever heard. Zosimus Sphere. As far as I understand it, they still own the place. You shouldn't go poking around in that old ditch, though. It's a death trap. How did you even know the old house was out there?"

Ashley leant forward and placed her hands on her knees. "Because we went there. We went inside the old farmhouse to explore. It's an overgrown ruin."

The old woman flinched. Jude noticed it, even though she

tried to hide it. She was unhappy that they'd visited the farm-house. But why would she care if she hadn't owned it in over half a century?

"There was somebody there," said Jude, deciding they might as well get to the point. There was no reason to beat around the bush with all the trouble they were in. "A woman named Rose."

This time the woman's reaction was impossible for her to disguise. She bucked in her chair and started wheezing. Immediately, Peter ran to her side. He picked up a glass of water from the side table and put it to the old woman's lips. "Grandma, are you okay?"

The old woman caught her breath and pushed her grandson out of the way. She looked through her spectacles at Jude and suddenly grew stern. She sat up in her recliner and stared them down. "Say that name to me again, lambies, so I'm sure I heard you right."

Jude saw the comprehension in the old woman's eyes. There was no memory loss or dementia there. She had the answers they sought; he was sure of it. He leant forward and returned the old woman's stony glare. "There was a naked woman in your fami-ly's old farmhouse. She was chained to the floor and surrounded by dead animals. She said her name was Rose."

The old woman broke her stare and slumped back in her chair. "You lambies don't know what you've done." She cleared her throat and shifted in her seat like she was struggling to get comfortable. "But I suppose you've come to the right place. You can call me Rita. Rose is my sister-in-law."

For a moment, Ashley didn't react. She retreated into her own mind and tried to make sense of what she'd heard. Rita and Rose were sisters-in-law, but Rita was ninety-six years old and Rose was nowhere near that. In fact, Rose had looked to be in her mid-thirties.

"I don't understand," said Jude. "You and Rose are family?"

Rita asked Peter to leave the room, and he did so obediently. Once he'd gone, Rita sighed. "I try not to involve Peter with the darkness that eats up the past. He's a good boy, pure of heart. Shame he's never found a kind woman to settle down with."

"Please," said Jude. "We need to know about Rose. She's... I'm not even sure how to say it."

"Oh, I know exactly what Rose is, lamby. She's a monster. If you two have had a run-in with her, I expect you already know that. You wouldn't be here otherwise."

Jude deflated. Ashley saw the relief on his face. Finally, they were speaking to someone who didn't think they were crazy.

Ashley asked, "Why was Rose chained up in your family's old farmhouse?"

Rita shivered, shoulders bony and uneven. "Because I put her there. In times I can barely remember."

Ashley raised an eyebrow. Rita didn't look strong enough to put anybody in chains against their will. "*You* chained her up? Why?"

"Because she murdered my brother and his children. They were Rose's children, too, as it goes, but she was never much of a mother."

Jude shook his head. He clearly had a thousand questions, but none made it out of his mouth.

Rita pulled the knitted patchwork up so that it covered her stomach. She scratched at her fuzzy chin and muttered something to herself. Then she looked Ashley in the eye. "I chained Rose up in 1948, same year I left my family's farm behind for good. I let nature reclaim it, and reclaim it nature did. You might say I helped the process along some."

Ashley frowned. "What does that mean? You planted trees?"

"Something like that. Anyway, before I tell you what I did to Rose, I should first tell you what *she* did to me. Like I said, she killed my brother, my niece, and my nephew. They were sweet lambies, and my brother were a decent man. If he'd lived, that farm would still be in our family today. It were his birthright.

Mine too, 'cept I never wanted it. Wanted it even less after what Rose done. I never liked her from the day he brought her home, that I swear. Within a year, she and my brother were married, and Rose got her greedy mitts on everything my family owned. My brother worked his poor 'ands to the bone, but Rose wanted more. Eventually, when she realised she couldn't have it, she looked elsewhere, started seeing the town's bank manager. Craven pig were as vainglorious as she was, and the two were far better suited than Rose and my brother ever were. Maybe if she'd met the bank manager first, the darkness of my past would be brighter. As things turned out, Rose decided she didn't want to be a wife to my brother or a mother to her children anymore, so one day, casually as you'd like, she stabbed the three of them to death and burned their bodies in the pigsties. She planned on marrying the bank manager and having my family's farm as dessert. Her only problem were me. I knew she'd done it – no doubt in my mind. Didn't take me more than a day to have her admit it."

Jude rejoined the conversation. "How did you ever get her to admit to something like that?"

"I have my ways. The land can provide more than just food, lambies, if you learn how to speak its language."

"I'm not following," said Jude.

"Me neither," said Ashley. "Tell us exactly what you mean."

Rita chuckled. Her tiny body rattled. "Suppose what I'm saying is that I'm a witch. My mother were too, and her mother before that. It's not exactly as you'd think – there's no eye of newt or silly love spells – but it's as real as the wind and the rain. To be a witch means to sacrifice a part of yourself in exchange for certain favours. There must always be a balance to everything, which is why, in the case of Rose, I were able to ask for a great deal of power. She took three people I cared about from this world. That left a lot of room to rebalance the scales."

Ashley smirked. "You're a witch? Prove it."

Rita rolled her eyes, more like a teenager than an elderly

woman. She pointed a crooked finger at Ashley and said, "That bruise on your nose. Your dad done that, yes? Hit you this very afternoon, he did."

Ashley gasped.

The old lady shrugged as though it was nothing. "Easy to read pain when it's so fresh. Am I right, lamby?"

"Yes! But how did you... How the fuck did you know that?"

"Because she's a witch," said Jude.

Rita nodded. "That I am, and I'll ask you not to soil the air in here, girl."

"Sorry."

"With all that's happened," said Jude. "You being a witch isn't so strange. I've always wondered if such things were real."

Rita smiled warmly at Jude. "You have an open heart. People might call that a weakness, but I don't. In fact, one day you might find it's your strength."

"Wait!" said Ashley. "Everything you're talking about happened when you were a young woman, right? We saw Rose in the farmhouse and she was in her thirties. It makes no sense."

"Rose is as old as I am, lamby."

"How can that be true?"

"Because it is. You see, once I got her confession, I dealt with her accordingly. My dear old ma helped me, although she were dead less than a year later from the grief."

Jude leant forward, eyes locked onto the old woman. "What did you do?"

"We invited the bank manager over to our farmhouse for dinner, pretended we wanted to talk about a loan. He were arrogant enough that he came. My mother slit his throat in the kitchen and we used his bones to make Rose's chains. We bound her to the very spot where she had murdered my brother. Then we forged a locket from copper and pig flesh and placed it around her neck with photographs of my niece and nephew so that she could never escape the truth of what she had done. Finally, after we pierced her flesh with the bones of her dead lover and cursed her with the image of her dead children, we trapped her inside the farmhouse using ancient spells passed down through our family for generations. A triangle, the strongest of all shapes, was painted on the ground with her paramour's blood. Finally, my mother and I used the last of our power to invoke nature to fall upon the farmhouse and keep people out. Over time, that magic has probably faded, but as extra protection, I sold the farm to an organisation that deals with... unfit properties, you might say."

Jude jolted. "You mean there's a company that buys haunted houses?"

"They think of themselves as caretakers. It's their job to make sure nobody goes inside places like my family's old farmhouse. Given the two of you, it looks like they failed, but I'll give them some credit, it's been more than fifty years. I always knew Rose would be discovered one day, but I only cared about making her suffer. The locket around her neck is cursed. It gives her eternal life. Eternal suffering. If I had just killed her, her wickedness would have been at an end, but my darkness demanded more. I let it win out over my conscience. Perhaps it's finally time for me to pay for my sins. Tell me, lambies, did you enter the triangle? Is Rose free?"

Ashley shook her head. "We didn't enter the triangle."

Rita exhaled. "Thank the Lord. The triangle is the only thing keeping her—"

"But someone else did."

Rita went rigid. Her eyes stretched wide. "Rose is unbound?"

Ashley swallowed a lump in her throat. The fear in the old woman's eyes was not comforting at all. "There was a girl named Lily Barnes. She went into the triangle. Rose killed her. She... she couldn't see Rose."

"Only the pure of flesh can see the wicked of heart. This girl, Lily, she was no longer a virgin?"

Ashley grimaced. "What? I don't know. Gross."

"She probably wasn't," said Jude. "She was kind of off the rails."

Rita exhaled again. She seemed to be growing tired, like continuing the conversation was hard work. "Only virgins, or those who have only ever known the body of a spouse, can see the likes of Rose. The locket around her neck pins her to the in-between, keeps her soul thinly bound to existence, never able to be truly alive and never able to pass on to the next. I admit, my revenge upon her was grave, and yet..."

"And yet what?" asked Jude.

"And yet to this day, I do not regret it. Perhaps I will pay for embracing such hatred. I fear the day may be soon."

"What do we do?" asked Ashley, not wanting to get side-tracked. She could see that Rita was losing focus. "How do we stop Rose?"

Rita shook her head. "I fear you cannot, lamby. To finally give Rose rest, one would need to obtain her locket and destroy it."

Ashley reached into her pocket and pulled out the locket. "You mean this one right here?"

Rita gasped and reached out a hand. "Give that to me! Let me see it!"

Ashley looked at Jude, unsure. Did they really want to hand over the one thing they had to a woman they barely knew? Did they trust Rita? Jude gave a subtle nod to suggest he did.

Ashley leant forward and handed over the locket. Rita took it carefully in her withered hands and stared at it like it was the world's finest diamond. She struggled with the clasp but eventually got it open. Tears came to her eyes.

"Those were your niece and nephew?" said Jude.

Rita nodded, although she kept her focus on the photographs inside the locket. "Yes. Elizabeth and George. Oh, how I miss them. I used to teach them nursery rhymes, dozens of 'em. Nowadays, I can barely remember the words to a single one. Age is a funny thing. Gets to a point where the past is unbelievably long and the future terrifyingly small. My days left on this Earth are few, but I'm glad to have lived this long." She looked at them and held the locket up so that it dangled from her fingers. "You must take this back and destroy it."

Ashley raised an eyebrow. "Yeah, okay. No problem. We can just throw it on the carriageway and wait for a lorry to drive over it, or burn it or something."

Rita shook her head. "You can't destroy this locket so easily. It's full of power. Not just the power that my mother and I placed inside it, but several decades of Rose's suffering. Pain and torment, over time, can grow into something real. Rose's hatred and anger are inside this locket. I can feel it."

Ashley grunted. "What, then? You said destroy it, so how do we do that?"

Rita looked her in the eye, her expression weary and possibly afraid. "The magic inside this locket can be undone only in the place it was forged. You must return it... to... to its birthplace and bury it beneath wood, stone... and flesh. Nature must reclaim it."

"What the fuck does that even mean?"

Rita wheezed and sat forward. She pointed a finger at Ashley and wagged it. "I... I told you, young lady... I..." She coughed and hacked, her frail body rattling on in the recliner. The door burst open and Peter hurried in. He went to his grandmother and started patting her on the back. Rita tried to push him away, but this time she was too weak. "S-Something is wrong," she moaned. "I... I feel her. Rose is here!"

"What do you need, Grandma? What should I do?"

Jude stood up from the sofa and started to fret. Ashley shuffled to the edge of the sofa cushions, expecting to be dismissed now that Rita had clearly grown tired and stressed. The locket had somehow found its way onto the floor. Rita must have dropped it. Ashley leant forward to reclaim it.

Rita reached an arm past her grandson and pointed at Jude. "You must leave here. You must leave before she finds you. The locket. Take it home. Destroy it. Destroy Rose like I *should have done a long time ago.*"

Ashley got to her feet and stared at Jude. He'd turned as white as a sheet, and she assumed she didn't look any better. They had come here seeking answers, but those they had received were frightening. Rose wasn't a witch or a monster. She was a remorseless killer trapped in place for over half a century, waiting for her chance to get free, and now Ashley had something of hers.

Rose will be coming for this locket.

And a moment later, she arrived.

CHAPTER SEVENTEEN

THE LAMPS in the room turned off, leading Ashley to realise it had grown dark outside. Things fell off the walls as if there was an earthquake, except the floor did not shake. Peter moved away from his grandmother and looked around. Rita remained in her lounger, deathly silent.

Jude looked around nervously. "What's happening?"

"She's here," said Rita. "She's come for her locket, the thing that gives her life eternal. You must go. You know what to do."

"Help us." Jude put his hands together in prayer. "Please."

"Go."

Peter turned to them, his cheerful demeanour completely gone. "I understand this is to do with my grandma's past, but she's an old lady now. She can't help you. You need to leave."

Ashley grabbed Jude by the arm. "Come on, we have to go." She moved over to the door, which had closed after Peter had rushed in. She opened it again and screamed.

Rose stood in the doorway, exactly as she had appeared in the farmhouse when Jude's camera had flashed – snakelike black hair down to her naked hips, and mesmerisingly green eyes. Grey patches of corpse-like skin covered her body in several places, and pulsing blue veins throbbed in her cheeks. Her ruined hands had somehow healed, but despite that, she was halfway between a living woman and a rotting cadaver. She reeked of evil. Rage and violence flowed from her in waves. It made Ashley's eyes water. She backed off, crashing up against Jude, and the two of them retreated to the edge of the small sitting room.

Peter turned to see what had startled them, and when he saw Rose, he gasped. He studied her nakedness for a split second and was clearly repulsed, then he threw up a hand and began to mutter something under his breath, some kind of chant. He obviously knew a certain amount of witchcraft himself.

But not enough.

Rose threw an arm out and struck Peter across the side of his face. The blow was so strong that it lifted him off his feet and sent him sprawling onto the sofa. Ashley turned, intending to help him get back up, but he was unconscious. Or worse.

Rose took another step, moving further into the room. She turned to Ashley and hissed like a snake, exposing her brown, rotting teeth. "Give it back to me," she whispered, her voice like a distant echo.

Ashley was so scared that she reached out the hand that was holding the locket and attempted to give it back. When Rose's eyes fell upon it, her thick red lips twisted into an unnatural facsimile of a smile. Maybe if she had the locket back, she would leave them alone.

Rita leapt out of her chair and stood up. She was a tiny thing, barely taller than a child. Her back was twisted and bony lumps covered her shoulders. All the same, she stepped in front of Rose and faced the abominable woman down. "I knew we'd meet again, sister-in-law. Your punishment has been long, yet utterly deserved. Let these lambies go. Let them put you to rest so that your suffering may finally be at an end. It is better than you deserve."

Rose snarled, her broken teeth grinding together and a grey worm-like tongue poking through the gaps. "I have waited.

Waited for this." She lifted a long-fingered hand in front of her face and snapped it closed into a fist.

Rita clutched her chest and moaned. "No... No, you must be stopped. Your evil... must be..."

Ashley yelped as the old woman collapsed to the ground at her feet. She wheezed and clawed at her chest while thick blue veins popped up all over her bulging neck.

Despite her suffering, Rita locked eyes with Ashley and spoke. "Go... before it's... too late."

Ashley looked at the locket in her hand and didn't know what to do. Should she stay and help the old lady? Or run?

Jude grabbed her wrist and the two of them took off, racing through the open door and exiting the house as quickly as they could. By the time they made it through the gate at the end of the driveway, they were both sobbing. Inside the house, they heard Peter screaming.

CHAPTER EIGHTEEN

IT WAS DARK, but not quite night. The sun had disappeared, replaced by the moon. The odd cloud still drifted overhead, barely visible against the dark blue sky, but there was not yet a single star. Half-an-hour, and night would settle in comfortably. It meant they would have to visit the farmhouse in the dark, which was not a pleasant thought.

Ashley had never run so far without a break in her life, and by the time she and Jude stopped, they were sweating profusely and struggling to breathe. They had made it just over halfway home and were walking alongside the main road. They had just passed the embankment full of daffodils, but this time they didn't stopp to pick any.

I think we just left two dead bodies behind us. Rose gave Rita a heart attack. How is that even possible?

And what about Peter? Is he okay?

Why is this happening?

Jude doubled over and heaved. For a moment, it looked like he was going to puke, but nothing came out except a mouthful of stringy saliva. Once he was done, he turned to Ashley with a grim expression on his face. "I... I don't know if I can go back to the farmhouse. I-I just want to go home, no matter the consequences. The police can pin everything on me and lock me up for life; I don't care."

"Yes, you do. If we have any chance of getting through this, we need to do what Rita told us. We need to destroy the locket and put Rose to rest. Otherwise, this will never end and more people are going to get hurt. We have to do this, Jude. Your whole life, you've wanted to go on an adventure, to be brave, so here's your chance. Rose is an evil, twisted bitch who murdered her own children, so let's do what Rita should've done in the first place and finish her. One down, two down, right? What type of person do you want to be?"

Jude took several laboured breaths, still winded. Several cars passed by and hit them with their headlights. After a couple of minutes, he straightened up and gave himself a shake. "Once again, the warrior princess shows no fear. Her trusted mage is honoured to be by her side."

Ashley shoved him playfully and smiled. "You're such a nerd. I love you, Jude. Thanks for being my friend all these years."

"No one else would have you," he said, chuckling, "but that's their loss."

"Damn straight!" She threw out her arms and kicked out a leg. "I'll remember you when I'm a famous backing dancer."

"Nice moves."

She did the robot, being silly and making him laugh. "You reckon I have what it takes?"

"Fuck yeah!"

Ashley was surprised by Jude's bad language. Usually he left the foul mouth stuff to her. She pulled him in for a cuddle and the two of them embraced for a full minute before getting going again in a rush. Rose could be anywhere, and if she caught up to them before they got to the farmhouse, there was no telling what she might do.

Maybe she'll stop our hearts in our chests like Rita's. Or maybe we'll put that bitch to rest once and for all.

This warrior princess is coming for you, Rose.

They reached the woods less than an hour later, and by then it was fully dark. Stepping into the trees with nothing except moonlight was terrifying, and every snapping twig and rustling insect set Ashley's teeth on edge. The hairs on the back of her neck came alive like caterpillars. Now and then she deliberately bumped against Jude just to feel him there. They were both silent, and she knew it was because they were thinking the same thing: that they might die out here tonight.

They made it to the top of Devil's Ditch and wasted no time in sliding down on their butts. They slid to the bottom and rolled back onto their feet with ease.

We're becoming professionals at this.

The trees and bushes were trampled, and there was an empty plastic water bottle lying on the ground. The police had obviously stormed through the area, but where were they now? Were they still searching for Lily, or had they given up?

"We need to make sure we're not seen," said Ashley. "The police could be out here."

Jude nodded. "When I tried to get help this morning, the woods seemed to fight me. It must have been Rita's spell. Maybe it will keep the police from hanging around."

"Maybe. Come on, let's do this."

A few minutes later, they passed the NO TRESPASSING sign. A minute after that, they were standing in the clearing and staring at the old farmhouse.

In the silvery moonlight, the farmhouse appeared ghost-like. The jagged shapes and sharp angles were unnatural among the trees and bushes, and Ashley sensed now how cursed the place was. It smelled of death and decay, and her skin tingled just being there. Something deep inside her mind – instinct, perhaps – told her to run, and screamed that she was in danger. It took several moments to override that fear.

The clearing was trampled, but there were no police officers around. They must have come, searched, and left. She imagined they were now searching the estate for Jude and Ashley.

Jude spoke. "Rita said we have to bury the locket beneath wood, stone, and flesh. Any ideas?"

Ashley strode forward into the clearing and stopped at a certain spot. She nodded at the floor where the rotting carcass of whatever animal Jude had stepped in was. "Here's our flesh. All we need now is wood and stone."

"Well, there's plenty of that about." Jude turned a circle and started kicking at the ground, sending leaves and twigs flying. He moved back towards the bushes where they had entered the clearing, and there he found a thick branch that he brought over. He threw it down next to the dead animal. "Two down, one to go."

There was a sudden chaotic uproar, and Ashley and Jude instinctively pressed against each other. The screeching came from everywhere as birds took flight from trees and small critters bolted through the bushes. Something had disturbed the wildlife. Ashley had a good idea what.

Rose appeared in the centre of the clearing, stone-still like a statue. The only parts of her that seemed alive were her bright green eyes that cut through the darkness like sparkling gemstones. Leaves and moss swirled around her feet as a cyclonic wind rose up from the ground. Then a full-on gale spiralled through the clearing.

Ashley shielded her face with an arm as airborne twigs, stones, and weeds pummelled her. She shouted out to Jude, "We need to bury the locket."

"How? She's here. She'll kill us."

Ashley dared to move her arm away from her face to look for Rose, but the woman had gone.

Ashley sensed movement to her left.

Rose was standing right beside her. She stank of rot and

decay. Parts of her flesh were hanging loose. Her bottom lip was split and bloody.

Jude shouted out a warning and pushed Ashley aside. By the time he turned to face Rose, she was already throwing an arm out to strike him. She caught him in the temple and sent him spinning to the ground.

Ashley cried out. "Jude! Jude, are you okay?"

He was dazed but managed to crawl away through the dirt and leaves. "I... I'm fine," he said. "Stay back from her, Ash."

He didn't need to tell her twice. Ashley hopped backwards and put distance between herself and Rose.

Rose gave another of her unnatural smiles, and the contents of the ground beneath her feet seemed to die. The moss and weeds shrivelled up and turned black. "Girl," she whispered. "I knew the moment I met you that you would be the one to free me. I visited you in the night, calling out for your return, and you did return. I see you. I see the darkness inside of you. The rage, it is exquisite. Let it feed."

Ashley continued backing away, moving towards the farm-house. "Fuck off, bitch."

Rose cackled. The sound echoed off every tree.

The gale continued to blow, making it hard to see or even move. It was like being struck by a horde of flies, small constant assaults all over Ashley's body – the twigs, stones, and everything else lifted into the air by Rose's fury. Barely any moonlight made it into the clearing.

There was movement at the centre of the clearing. Rose wasn't pursuing Ashley, but she continued to cackle. Ashley fought the urge to just plain run the hell out of there. Jude was back on his feet fifteen metres away, but still dazed. In the centre of the clearing, a new person appeared, someone with wild, frizzy hair right down to her waist.

Lily. What the fuck?

Lily appeared out of the darkness and staggered towards Jude with jerky, inhuman movements. She was a puppet pulled along on uneven strings. Her eyes were ruby red and her mouth was a massive, cavernous hole. She appeared to have no teeth, but her tongue was three times the length it should've been. It flapped around and licked the air.

"Little help here," Jude cried out.

Rose was standing between Ashley and Jude, but Ashley desperately wanted to be at her friend's side. If this was how they died, then they should do it together. So, using an athleticism she hadn't even known she had, she dodged to the side and spun around Rose. Then, with some space, she raced to Jude's side. He grabbed her arm and squeezed it tightly, almost like he was checking to see if she was real. "We need stone," he said. "We have to finish this."

Ashley nodded. If there was any way out of this, it was by doing what Rita had told them to do. They needed to bury the locket. "You find some stone. I'll deal with Lily."

To her own astonishment, Ashley took herself towards Lily. The vicious bully was now a shambling zombie – or a human slug – and there was no way she could still be alive. Rose had corrupted and reanimated her corpse. It couldn't have happened to a nicer person, but Ashley still pitied her former tormentor. There was no intelligence in Lily's glowing red eyes, and her twisted body looked like it had been forged from agony itself.

"Always thought it would be me that killed you," said Ashley. "Guess I'll have to satisfy myself with killing you the second time."

Lily jerked towards her, quicker than expected. She made no sound except a strangled moaning noise. She reached out for Ashley, but Ashley ducked beneath her outstretched hands. Then she turned and threw a punch, striking Lily in the centre of the chest and sending her ghoulish body stumbling backwards. Ashley grimaced as her fist returned to her caked in gore. She wiped herself on her T-shirt and spat in disgust.

It's literally like hitting a corpse.

Ashley glanced over her shoulder to see Jude scurrying

around near the bushes. He needed to hurry the hell up and find some stone.

Does it need to be a big stone? Or will any do?

This is so fucked up.

Lily came at Ashley again. This time, she moved even more quickly. She caught Ashley across the cheek with a clawed hand, and Ashley sensed blood on her face for the second time that day. Familiar rage bubbled up inside of her, and she clenched her fists and gritted her teeth. Without thinking, she lashed out and kicked Lily in the stomach. Lily doubled over. She quickly straightened up, but her torso was distorted, broken and damaged where her foot had landed. Lily's body was barely held together, but she appeared to feel no pain. She struck Ashley again, this time on the other cheek. Blood poured down her face.

"You. Fucking. Bitch!" Ashley bellowed in rage. Lily had terrorised her for the best part of three years, and she was still doing it now after she was dead. She was tired of people pushing her around and making her feel bad just for being who she was. Why didn't the world just fuck off? What was so bad about just being Ashley?

Lily raised a hand to strike again, but before she did, her head came apart like a dandelion. Scraps of flesh and bone floated away on the wind, and her headless corpse toppled backwards to rejoin the earth. Ashley gasped. She reached into her pocket and pulled out the locket, knowing it had just made her wishes come true.

No, not my wishes. My anger. It made my anger come true. I can feel Rose's hatred inside it.

Ashley turned to check on Jude but found Rose standing directly in front of her. She raised her hands, which had turned into sharpened claws. She hissed, a narrow tongue like a strip of beef jerky flicking out between her bleeding lips. "Give me what is mine."

Ashley cowered, too terrified to move.

Jude raced to her side and quickly got Rose's attention before she swiped a claw at Ashley's exposed throat. "Hey, bitch, you've got something behind your ear." He reached out and punched Rose right in the side of the head. Then he pulled his arm back to reveal his gold plastic coin. "You're a real treasure."

Ashley broke out of her terror enough to groan. "I always knew you were made of money. Seriously, Jude, we went over this."

Jude groaned. "Damn it!"

Rose's head snapped back into place, and she grabbed Jude around the throat so quickly that he never even made a move. His eyes bulged in his head and he started to gag. The gold coin fell from his hand and landed in the mud.

Rose scowled. "Men made this world, but it is for women to inherit. We must give birth to our power and make manifest our rage. We shall not be servants and whores any longer."

"What do you want?" Ashley cried. "Please, just leave him alone."

Rose tossed Jude to the ground, where he lay choking. She whirled on Ashley, her green eyes pulsing. "I want it all. I want everything the world can give me. Power. It is intoxicating. Return what is mine and I shall reward you, girl. You feel powerless, but I can change that. Give me the locket and see your hopes and dreams realised."

Ashley looked at the piece of jewellery that was threaded between her fingers. It was open, and inside she could see the photographs of Rose's dead children. Rita had made the locket to punish Rose, to keep her trapped forever, but Ashley realised now that it had also benefited the child murderer. "You can never die if you're wearing this, can you? That's why you want it back."

"Yessss. Rita's curse is a gift. Now that I am no longer bound by Gaia's triangle, I am free to leave this place. But without the locket, my time is short. Give it to me, girl, and I shall see all your wishes come true. I shall share my power with you and help you harness that burning oil searing your veins. We are women; we are powerful. Be my daughter in this."

Ashley imagined what it would be like to be powerful. Rose had torn Lily Barnes apart like a child pulled apart a spider. To have such power, to be so unafraid... it seemed impossible.

Can Rose really give me power? Could I be like her? Could I tear apart my tormentors without breaking a sweat? No more beatings from bullies like Lily Barnes.

Or my dad.

I could be powerful. I could be strong.

Rose was grinning, her broken teeth glinting in the strangled moonlight. She reached out a skeletal hand to Ashley, begging for the locket. Ashley held it up in the air between them, making her mind up about what to do.

Power.

I want it.

Jude called out to her from the ground. "Ash! Get away from her. Throw me the locket. We need to bury it."

"Silence, boy!" Rose hissed and stretched out an arm. A bloody gash opened across Jude's cheek and he grabbed his face, screaming. Rose looked back at Ashley and sneered. "Be my daughter in this. Say the word and I will show you what real power is. I'll show you what women like you and I can do to men like him. Give me the locket, girl."

Ashley was still holding the locket up in the air. Seeing Jude hurt was unexpectedly satisfying. Anger filled her as she recalled the many times he hadn't stood up for himself. He was weak and she was strong. She had always been the strong one. Perhaps he deserved to die. The rage inside her almost demanded it.

All these years, he's been holding me down.

One down, two down.

How strong could I be without him?

She saw something glinting in the mud at her feet. A silly gold plastic coin. Part of Jude's dorky, childish magic tricks.

Ashley knew what she needed to do. She grinned at Rose and offered the locket. "Here, take it."

Rose grinned, her lips splitting apart and bleeding. "Yesss."

But just as Rose reached out to take the locket, Ashley yanked it away with a shimmy of her arm. She followed it up with a spin and a kick that would have made Michael Jackson proud. "Think I'll pass on being your kid, Rose. I don't want to end up like your last ones." With that, she pulled the locket up and over her head and let it fall onto her chest. Immediately she felt a burning sensation, even through her T-shirt. Her fists clenched in agony and her jaw set tightly. Her entire body cried out in pain.

Then the pain stopped.

Fury flowed through Ashley's veins, but for once it was comforting. It no longer had control of her. She had control of *it*.

Rose's mouth opened wide and the decayed flesh of her diseased body turned jet black. Her rotten teeth fell out one by one, as did her hair.

With a shrug of her shoulders, Ashley said, "Fuck off and die, bitch."

"Fool!" Rose spoke between mouthfuls of thick black tar. "Wretched little bitch. I... I see you. I see your heart and it is putrescent. There is no victory in this for you. I shall seize you in your nightmares and squeeze your insides until you pop. Every night, I shall... I shall be with you. Stupid... child." She reached out to snatch the locket, but Ashley kicked the weakened woman in the leg and sent her to her knees.

"Stay down. It's over."

Rose glared, but something in her eyes made it obvious that she knew she was finished – she was afraid. As a final defiant act, the dying woman threw out her arms like Christ on the cross and stared up at the night sky. "Let the devil take me, but no man will shall own me. I shall make Hell tremble."

Rose's body burst apart and scattered on the wind. In a second, she was gone, her evil finally at an end.

Ashely bent over and took deep breaths, her heart thudding against her chest.

It's over.

I did it. I beat her.

The oppressive air of the clearing went away, leaving behind only the pure scent of the woods. The moon grew brighter above the treetops.

Jude stood nearby, clutching his face and moaning. Blood covered his face, but he was relieved when he looked at her.

She picked up his plastic coin from the mud and took it over to him. Seeing it on the ground had reminded her of how innocent and pure her best friend was. He lived in a world where magic was only pretend and was supposed to put smiles on people's faces and make life a little more fun. He wasn't a coward or a wimp. Jude was a kind and gentle soul who had the strength to say no to anger. The Rickys, Lilys, and Roses of the world would never be enough to change him. He would never sink to their level by letting in anger and violence.

And if it wasn't for him, my anger would take over me and I would have nothing good left inside me. I need Jude, because without him, I'm alone.

Jude took his muddy coin and examined it. "Thanks, but I think I've had enough of magic."

She cupped a hand against his wounded cheek. His blood was hot against her palm. "Let's never come to these fucking woods again, yeah?"

Jude nodded seriously. "The warrior princess and her trusted mage agree to retire. Never again will they dare the perils of Devil's Ditch."

The two of them shared a laugh, but then Ashley noticed something that wasn't funny at all. When she pulled her hand away from Jude's bloody cheek, his wound had miraculously healed.

. . .

Jude was still hurting, so he had to lean on Ashley as they made their way out of Devil's Ditch. It was late, but his watch was cracked and broken, so he had no idea how late. For now, he was happy to enjoy the gentle breeze on his face and the complete silence of the woods as they trudged through the undergrowth.

The woods felt different now. He had never realised before how thick the air had been, but he could breathe deeply now. There was no scent to the air, and the trees and bushes swayed gently. Ashley's hand was on his back beneath his T-shirt. Her touch was hot and it soothed his aches. They both knew what they were walking into, but he was glad they were doing it together. "Ashley?"

"Yeah?"

"What happened back there? How did you beat Rose?" He also wanted to ask how she had healed his cheek, but he could only think about one thing at a time.

Ashley didn't answer for a moment. Then she removed her hand from his back and placed it around the locket on her chest. "Rita told us that decades of Rose's hate and anger were inside this locket and that it has power. I used it as a weapon and sent it back at Rose."

Jude kind of understood. It was clear that the locket had power – he had seen it when Ashley had destroyed Ricky's hand – but its main ability seemed to be hurting people. "Maybe you should take it off now."

She nodded. "As soon as we're out of here and safe, it's the first thing I'll be doing. I can feel it on me. It's like having a hot coal against my skin."

"It's evil," said Jude.

"Maybe, but it saved our butts, so I'm keeping it until I know we're outta the woods." She nudged him and smiled. "Get it? Outta the woods."

He grinned, but he couldn't manage a chuckle. "So what do you think comes next?"

"Probably the worst telling off of our lives followed by a lifetime grounding. The police, my dad, your mum; they're going to rip us to shreds."

"I'm not looking forward to any of it. It's going to suck, big time."

She put her hand back under his T-shirt and rubbed. "Yep, but then it'll be over. They can't punish us forever, and whatever happens, you and I will always know the truth. Nobody is ever going to keep us apart, Jude. One down, two down."

He nodded. "One down, two down."

"I think I see the footpath. Thank God. Let's put this place behind us."

"Yeah. I'm starving. Maybe we can manage to get something to eat before the police find us."

Ashley smirked at him. "I bet we can."

The police found them as soon as they left the woods.

CHAPTER NINETEEN

Jude lay back in Ashley's bed and stared at the ceiling. It was the last day of summer and school started tomorrow. With everything that had happened, he was more than thrilled to go back. Suddenly, maths lessons and Shakespeare were more enticing than they'd ever been. He couldn't wait to be bored.

In the ten days since they'd dealt with Rose, things had first got worse and then slowly got better. PC Riaz questioned them relentlessly about Lily Barnes, popping by each morning to get answers. No one had seen the girl in over a week, and no body had been located. Her family was on the warpath, and they wouldn't stop until they drew blood. Ashley and Jude did everything they could to stay out of the family's way, and fortunately, the police hadn't shared their names. If it ever got out that he and Ashley were the ones who had reported Lily's death, though, they would probably have to go into hiding.

As much as PC Riaz had been left irritated, confused, and eventually angry, he could not find any evidence of a crime. In the end, he had given both Ashley and Jude an official caution, and threatened them with a full-on prosecution if he heard one more word about a farmhouse in the woods. Funnily enough, the farmhouse itself no longer existed. Zosimus Sphere, the company that owned it, had moved in with equipment to flatten it. Jude hadn't gone into the woods, but there were caterpillar tracks all the way through it where a bulldozer had driven in, and he had seen the bricks and timbers being removed by a tractor and trailer.

The saddest part of the last week and a half was when Jude had opened the local paper and read about a freak incident in the posh part of town. A ninety-six-year-old woman had suffered a heart attack at the exact same moment as her forty-year-old grandson. Neighbours found them both dead, lying side by side.

Peter and Rita Glendale, just two more casualties from Jude and Ashley's actions.

Jude struggled with the guilt more than Ashley did. In fact, a weight seemed to have lifted from her shoulders, and she was happier and more confident than ever. She kept reminding him that Rose was the only person to blame for what had happened, and that they'd had no way of knowing the consequences when Lily and Ricky had chased them into the woods. He knew she was right, but he still kept thinking about all the misery their actions had caused.

Ashley entered her bedroom and sat on the bed beside Jude. He'd been waiting while she took a shower, and they planned on watching a film together. Then they were going to have an early night, ready for school. She leant over him now in only a bath towel. Her dark hair was wet and dripping. "What you thinking about?" she asked.

He moved up onto his elbows and looked at her. Her face was close to his, uncomfortably so. "Just about school. I'm looking forward to it. It'll be good to put this summer behind us, don't you think?"

She shrugged. "It hasn't been so bad. I feel like we can deal with anything now. People at school won't know what's hit 'em once we're through with them. This is *our* time now, Jude. No more being pushed around or bullied. I'm done with that. I doubt Ricky would even come near me after what I did to his hand."

He nodded. "That was... pretty rough. You think his hand will heal?"

"Who gives a shit? He's never going to mess with us again."

"I suppose you're right. I'm just glad you and I are still friends after everything that happened."

"Friends?" She chuckled. "Is that what you think we are? After everything that happened?"

He frowned, not knowing what she meant, and flinched when she moved her face right up against his. He went to object, but his words were cut off by her tongue probing into his mouth.

She's kissing me. Ashley is kissing me.

He was deeply uncomfortable for a moment, but then something took over him. All of a sudden, they were making out on her bed.

Is this happening?

Jude felt a rapidly growing bulge in his jeans, and when Ashley reached down and fondled it, he groaned. Then she was pulling at his clothes and throwing off her bath towel. She climbed on top of him. His hands slid over her silky thighs and up to her large breasts. Rose's locket hung around her neck. She had refused to take it off, even after he'd begged. She called it her trophy. After a few days, he had stopped nagging her and just forgotten about it. Other than her newfound confidence, she was the same old Ashley.

Except she's naked and on top of me.

She's so beautiful. Why have I not seen how beautiful she is before?

The next ten minutes flew by in a breathtaking, emotional whirl. Afterwards, Jude wanted to cry and shout triumphantly at the same time. He wanted to tell Ashley how much he loved her, but he couldn't get his thoughts in order. She was his friend. Like a sister.

No, not a sister. Not anymore.

What is happening?

Ashley remained sitting on top of him with a mischievous smile on her face while he went soft inside her. "Still think we're just friends?"

"I... I don't know what just happened. It was... amazing."

"Yeah, it was. Like I said, this is *our* time now. Nobody's gunna tell us what to do. We have the power now, Jude. I..."

He frowned. "What?"

"I love you. Always have, I guess. Just took a naked child killer in the woods to make me realise it."

He was shocked, and at the same time, not in the least surprised. He nodded. "Yeah, I love you too. There could never have been anyone else."

She kissed him on the mouth. He ran his hand behind her ear like he was going to pull out a coin, but instead he brought his fingers back along her cheek and stroked her face. "You're a treasure."

The door to Ashley's bedroom opened and her father stepped inside. It looked like he'd been about to say something, but when he saw his naked daughter sitting on top of an equally naked Jude, his face broke apart in anger and he raced forward. He grabbed Ashley by the hair and threw her to the floor. Jude tried to get up off the bed, but Ashley's dad struck him in the face and knocked him back down on the mattress. "I'll kill you," he snarled. "You do this in my house?"

Jude closed his eyes in fear as Ashley's father raised his fists to pummel him again.

"Leave him alone!" Ashley bellowed in a voice Jude had never heard her use before. It was so... angry.

Jude opened his eyes to watch what was happening and saw Ashley's dad turn away from him to face his daughter. Ashley was bleeding from her mouth. It stained her teeth, turning them red as she snarled like a wolf.

"You're never seeing this boy again," her father raged. "And you're grounded for life. Do you know how disrespectful this is? Under my roof!"

Ashley didn't appear afraid or at all ashamed. She stood before her father, completely naked, with her fists clenched. "Get. The. Fuck. Out. Of. My. Room."

"You dare speak to me like that?" Her dad raised a hand and took a step towards her.

Then he dropped like a sack of potatoes.

Ashley's dad lay on the floor, clutching his chest and groaning. The anger left him, and suddenly his eyes were wide and desperate. He reached out a hand to Ashley and tried to speak. He could only whimper.

Ashley clutched the locket against her chest and growled. "Nobody hits me. Nobody."

Jude sat up on the bed. He was aware he was naked, yet it was unimportant right now. "Ashley... stop!"

Her dad tried to get up, but it was a hopeless battle. The life left his eyes and he collapsed onto his back. He went still.

No question, he was dead.

Jude collapsed onto his side in shock. "Ash..."

Ashley's mum came rushing into the room. She looked around for a moment, confused, and then when she saw her husband lying on the floor, she dropped onto her knees and started screaming. She shook him over and over again, and wailed at Ashley to get help. But Ashley just stood there with a satisfied grin on her face.

Jude realised then that Ashley had changed. The anger that had always been inside her was now an ugly, dangerous thing. It was a weapon she could wield to hurt people. Sixty-odd years of Rose's hatred and malice was now hanging around her neck and infecting her with its evil. Strengthening her. Jude had known it the night in the clearing when she had healed the deep wound on his cheek. Part of him had also known it when she had refused to take off Rose's locket.

She likes the power.

And now she's killed her dad.

Jude looked at his best friend and tried to hold back tears. Blood trickled down Ashley's lip and some of it dripped onto her naked breasts. She was still staring at her dad, pleased by what she'd done.

He tried to get her attention. "Ash? Ashley, we need to get help. Your dad..."

She whirled on him, fury in her expression. It took several seconds for her to relax, and he found himself fearing her terribly. His heart thudded, and he wondered if she would ever make it stop beating in his chest.

"It's too late," she told him. "He's already dead. He'll never hurt me again."

Her mum stopped screaming and looked up at Ashley with a mixture of anger and confusion. "What are you talking about? He's your father. Ashley, please, just call for help."

Jude sat up on the bed again. "She's right. Ashley, we need to do something."

"He's dead." She spoke without emotion. "It's too late."

And Jude realised she was right. It *was* too late. Ashley was gone.

"Ashley...?" He shook his head. "Ash."

She narrowed her eyes at him and her upper lip curled slightly. "Don't turn on me, Jude. Not you."

"I-I need to go."

She smirked. "Shag and go, is that it?"

"What, no, of course not. I just..."

She motioned to the door. "Just go."

"I'll call you later."

"You'd better."

Jude put his clothes on rapidly, fled the bedroom, ran down the stairs, and rushed out of the front door. He broke into a run that didn't stop until he reached the playground, where he collapsed against the railings before guiding himself unsteadily to the bench. There, he sat and tried to catch his breath. Ashley was a killer, and the worst part was that she didn't even seem to care. In fact, she had enjoyed watching her father die at her feet.

We made love. She made love to me.

I can reach her. I can get her to take off the locket.

No, she will never agree to it. The power, it's inside her now, corrupting her. She'll never let it go. She won't stop. People around her are going to get hurt.

"Hey, Jude. You okay?"

Jude flinched. Ricky Dalca was walking towards him, his hand covered in bandages and a nasty bruise around his left eye. He actually smiled and called Jude by his actual name instead of calling him Judy, which was unnerving.

"Ricky? Um, what's up?"

He shrugged and took a seat on the bench beside Jude. "Nuffin' much. I'm actually looking forward to school. My last year before I have to get a job. Might as well enjoy it, aye?"

"Yeah. Have you heard anything about, um...?"

Ricky shook his head. "Lily's family has been knocking around, asking questions, but so far they haven't got any answers." He motioned to his bruised eye socket. "This was their work. I reckon the twins know I had something to do with Lily disappearing, but they haven't said anything yet. If they do, then I'm probably a dead man. Guess I'll just have to wait and see what happens." He leant forward, elbows on his knees. His bandages seemed small, like his hand was still withered and crippled beneath. "My head's a mess, man. Did all that shit really go down?"

Jude's mind rewound and started playing every tiny event from the moment he and Ashley had gone to spit on cars from the overpass. It seemed like a lifetime ago now. He nodded. "Yeah, it went down, but it's over now. More or less. It's just something we're going to have to live with. Maybe that's what growing up is."

Ricky chuckled, but it was a sad sound. "Trying to cover up

dodgy shit so you don't go to prison or end up in a shallow grave? Sounds like growing up is going to fucking suck. Hey, where's Ashley? You two not joined at the hip today?"

Jude felt tears coming and had to fight them. "I think it's time I find out who I am without her. I miss her already, but I'm kind of looking forward to a future where everything's different. She and I used to have this saying, one down, two down. It meant we always had each other's back. I have a new saying now."

Ricky raised an eyebrow. "Oh?"

"Yeah. One day, two day. Because that's how I'm going to take things from now on. One day at a time."

"Sounds like a good plan, mate. Maybe I'll follow it myself." He let out a sigh, like his good mood had taken energy he no longer had. He lifted his bandaged hand so that Jude could see it. "She did this to me, didn't she? I'm not sure how, but it was her, right?"

Jude wasn't sure what to say for a moment. He decided on the truth. "Yeah, she did that to you. Ashley's dangerous."

"Yeah, I get that. Think you're best off keeping your distance." He straightened up on the bench and sighed. "I'm sorry for being a dick to you all these years, man. You wanna be mates?"

Jude turned and nodded. "Yeah, I'd like that, Ricky. Hey, do you like magic?"

"Nah, man. I fucking hate it."

"Me too." Jude stood up from the bench and looked at his new friend. "I'll see you tomorrow at school."

Ricky smiled weakly. "I'll probably be late, but yeah, I'll see you there. Think I might even try and learn something this year. One day, two day, right?"

Jude smiled. "One day, two day."

Jude said goodbye again, and then walked home alone, wondering how much more magic was in the world.

And if it was all evil.

The trusted mage has lost his princess to the darkness, but he is ready for whatever comes next. It is time for a new adventure and the world needs heroes.

Jude managed a smile.

WANT FREE BOOKS?

Don't miss out on your FREE Iain Rob Wright horror pack. Five terrifying books sent straight to your inbox.

No strings attached & signing up is a doddle.

Just Visit IainRobWright.com

ALSO BY IAIN ROB WRIGHT

Iain Rob Wright is one of the UK's most successful horror and suspense writers, with novels including the critically acclaimed, THE FINAL WINTER; the disturbing bestseller, ASBO; and the wicked screamfest, THE HOUSEMATES.

His work is currently being adapted for graphic novels, audio books, and foreign audiences. He is an active member of the Horror Writer Association and a massive animal lover.

www.iainrobwright.com
FEAR ON EVERY PAGE

For more information
www.iainrobwright.com
author@iainrobwright.com

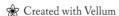